In Focus 英語閱讀

活用五大關鍵技巧

作者 Owain Mckimm
Zachary Fillingham
Shara Dupuis
Richard Luhrs

譯者 劉嘉珮

審訂 Richard Luhrs

Contents Chart 目錄

Introduction 簡介

本套書依程度共分四冊，專為初中級讀者編寫。每冊包含50篇閱讀文章、30餘種文體與題材。各冊分級主要針對文章字數多寡、字級難易度、文法深淺、句子長度來區分。生活化的主題配合多元化的體裁，讓讀者透過教材，體驗豐富多樣的語言學習經驗，提昇學習興趣，增進學習效果。

字數（每篇）	國中 1200 單字（每篇）	國中 1201-2000 單字（每篇）	高中 7000 (3, 4, 5 級)（每篇）	文法程度	句子長度
Book 1 120–150	93%	7 字	3 字	（國一） first year	15 字
Book 2 150–180	86%	15 字	6 字	（國二） second year	18 字
Book 3 180–210	82%	30 字	7 字	（國三） third year	25 字
Book 4 210–250	75%	50 字	12 字	（國三進階） advanced	28 字

本書架構

閱讀文章

本套書涵蓋豐富且多元的主題與體裁。文章形式廣泛蒐羅各類生活中常見的實用體裁，包含短文、論壇、問卷、宣傳手冊、海報、網站、廣告等三十餘種，以日常相關的生活經驗為重點編寫設計，幫助加強基礎閱讀能力，提升基本英語溝通能力，為基礎生活英語紮根。

收錄大量題材有趣、多元且生活化的短文，範圍囊括青少年生活、學校、自然、藝術與人文、社會行為、體育、動物、趣聞、健康與身體、娛樂等三十餘種，主題多元化且貼近生活經驗，可激起學生學習興趣，協助學生理解不同領域知識。

閱讀測驗

每篇短文後，皆接有五題閱讀理解選擇題，評量學生對文章的理解程度。閱讀測驗所訓練學生的閱讀技巧包括：

- 文章中心思想（Main Idea）／主題（Subject Matter）
- 支持性細節（Supporting Details）
- 從上下文猜測字義（Words in Context）
- 文意推論（Making Inferences）
- 看懂影像圖表（Visualizing Comprehension）

文章中心思想（Main Idea）

閱讀文章時，讀者可以試著問自己：「**作者想要傳達什麼訊息？**」透過審視理解的方式，檢視自己是否了解文章意義。

文章主題（Subject Matter）

這類問題幫助讀者專注在所閱讀的文章中，在閱讀文章前幾行後，讀者應該問自己：「**這篇文章是關於什麼？**」這麼做能幫助你立刻集中注意力，快速理解文章內容，進而掌握整篇文章脈絡。

支持性細節（Supporting Details）

每篇文章都是由細節組成來支持主題句。「**支持性細節**」包括範例、說明、敘述、定義、比較、對比和比喻。

從上下文猜測字義（Words in Context）

由上下文猜生字意義，是英文閱讀中一項很重要的策略。弄錯關鍵字詞的意思會導致誤解作者想要傳達的觀點。

文意推論（Making Inferences）

推論性的問題會要讀者歸納文章中已有的資訊，來思考、推理，並且將線索連結起來，推論可能的事實，這種問題的目的是訓練讀者的批判性思考和邏輯性。

看懂影像圖表（Visualizing Comprehension）

這類問題考驗讀者理解視覺資料的能力，包括表格、圖片、地圖等，或是索引、字典，學會運用這些圖像資料能增進你對文章的整體理解。

How Do I Use This Book? 使用導覽

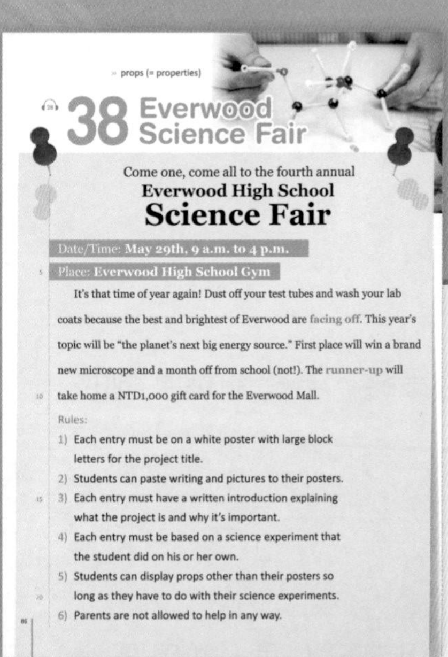
props (= properties)

38 Everwood Science Fair

Come one, come all to the fourth annual
Everwood High School
Science Fair

Date/Time: **May 29th, 9 a.m. to 4 p.m.**

Place: **Everwood High School Gym**

It's that time of year again! Dust off your test tubes and wash your lab coats because the best and brightest of Everwood are facing off. This year's topic will be "the planet's next big energy source." First place will win a brand new microscope and a month off from school (not!). The runner-up will take home a NTD1,000 gift card for the Everwood Mall.

Rules:

1) Each entry must be on a white poster with large block letters for the project title.
2) Students can paste writing and pictures to their posters.
3) Each entry must have a written introduction explaining what the project is and why it's important.
4) Each entry must be based on a science experiment that the student did on his or her own.
5) Students can display props other than their posters so long as they have to do with their science experiments.
6) Parents are not allowed to help in any way.

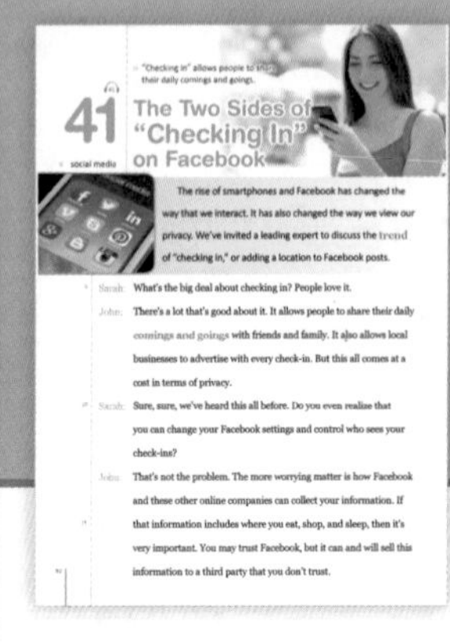
"Checking in" allows people to share their daily comings and goings.

41 The Two Sides of "Checking In" on Facebook

social media

The rise of smartphones and Facebook has changed the way that we interact. It has also changed the way we view our privacy. We've invited a leading expert to discuss the trend of "checking in," or adding a location to Facebook posts.

Sarah: What's the big deal about checking in? People love it.

John: There's a lot that's good about it. It allows people to share their daily comings and goings with friends and family. It also allows local businesses to advertise with every check-in. But this all comes at a cost in terms of privacy.

Sarah: Sure, sure, we've heard this all before. Do you even realise that you can change your Facebook settings and control who sees your check-ins?

John: That's not the problem. The more worrying matter is how Facebook and these other online companies can collect your information. If that information includes where you eat, shop, and sleep, then it's very important. You may trust Facebook, but it can and will sell this information to a third party that you don't trust.

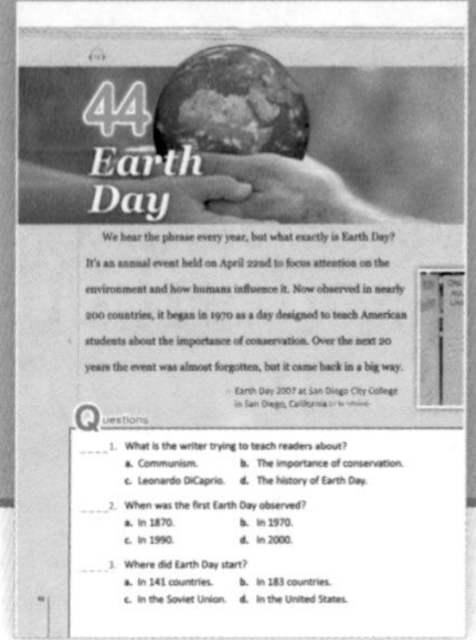
44 Earth Day

We hear the phrase every year, but what exactly is Earth Day? It's an annual event held on April 22nd to focus attention on the environment and how humans influence it. Now observed in nearly 200 countries, it began in 1970 as a day designed to teach American students about the importance of conservation. Over the next 20 years the event was almost forgotten, but it came back in a big way.

Earth Day 2007 at San Diego City College in San Diego, California

Questions

1. What is the writer trying to teach readers about?
   a. Communism. b. The importance of conservation. c. Leonardo DiCaprio. d. The history of Earth Day.
2. When was the first Earth Day observed?
   a. In 1870. b. In 1970. c. In 1990. d. In 2000.
3. Where did Earth Day start?
   a. In 141 countries. b. In 183 countries. c. In the Soviet Union. d. In the United States.

主題多元化

題材有趣且多元，貼近日常生活經驗，包含青少年生活、自然、藝術與人文、體育、動物、趣聞、健康與身體、娛樂等，激發學生學習興趣，協助學生理解不同領域知識。

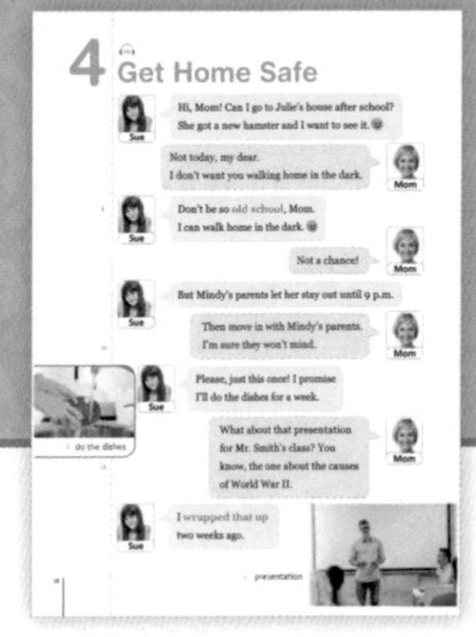
4 Get Home Safe

Sue: Hi, Mom! Can I go to Julie's house after school? She got a new hamster and I want to see it.

Mom: Not today, my dear. I don't want you walking home in the dark.

Sue: Don't be so old school, Mom. I can walk home in the dark.

Mom: Not a chance!

Sue: But Mindy's parents let her stay out until 9 p.m.

Mom: Then move in with Mindy's parents. I'm sure they won't mind.

Sue: Please, just this once! I promise I'll do the dishes for a week.

Mom: What about that presentation for Mr. Smith's class? You know, the one about the causes of World War II.

Sue: I wrapped that up two weeks ago.

do the dishes

presentation

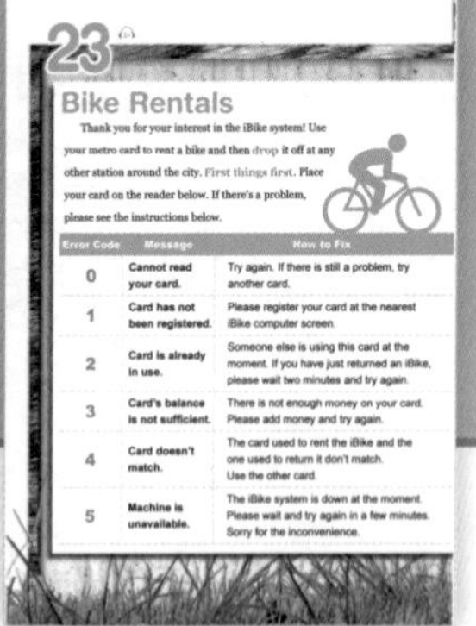
23 Bike Rentals

Thank you for your interest in the iBike system! Use your metro card to rent a bike and then drop it off at any other station around the city. First things first. Place your card on the reader below. If there's a problem, please see the instructions below.

Error Code	Message	How to Fix
0	Cannot read your card.	Try again. If there is still a problem, try another card.
1	Card has not been registered.	Please register your card at the nearest iBike computer screen.
2	Card is already in use.	Someone else is using this card at the moment. If you have just returned an iBike, please wait two minutes and try again.
3	Card's balance is not sufficient.	There is not enough money on your card. Please add money and try again.
4	Card doesn't match.	The card used to rent the iBike and the one used to return it don't match. Use the other card.
5	Machine is unavailable.	The iBike system is down at the moment. Please wait and try again in a few minutes. Sorry for the inconvenience.

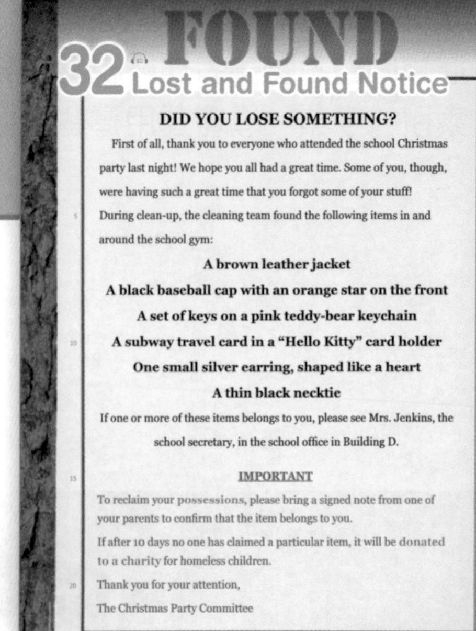
FOUND

32 Lost and Found Notice

DID YOU LOSE SOMETHING?

First of all, thank you to everyone who attended the school Christmas party last night! We hope you all had a great time. Some of you, though, were having such a great time that you forgot some of your stuff! During clean-up, the cleaning team found the following items in and around the school gym:

A brown leather jacket
A black baseball cap with an orange star on the front
A set of keys on a pink teddy-bear keychain
A subway travel card in a "Hello Kitty" card holder
One small silver earring, shaped like a heart
A thin black necktie

If one or more of these items belongs to you, please see Mrs. Jenkins, the school secretary, in the school office in Building D.

IMPORTANT

To reclaim your possessions, please bring a signed note from one of your parents to confirm that the item belongs to you.

If after 10 days no one has claimed a particular item, it will be donated to a charity for homeless children.

Thank you for your attention,
The Christmas Party Committee

體裁多樣化

廣納生活中常見的實用體裁，包含短文、論壇、問卷、宣傳手冊、海報、網站、廣告等，以日常相關生活經驗設計編寫，為基礎生活英語紮根。

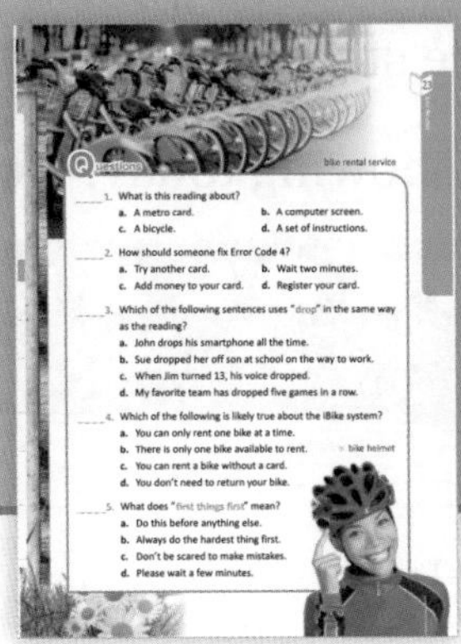

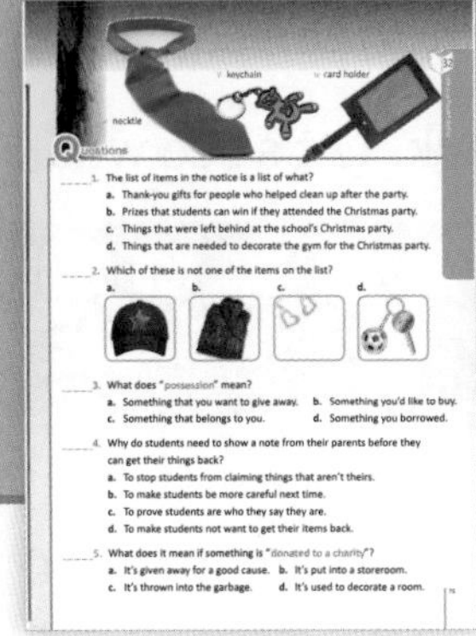

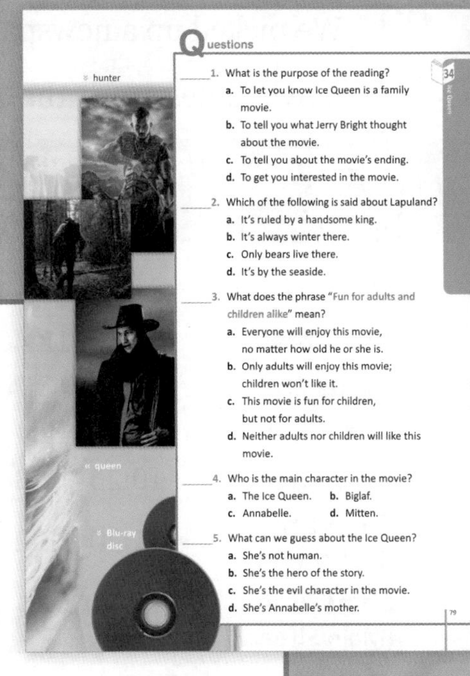

閱讀技巧練習題

左頁文章、右頁測驗的設計方式，短文後皆接有五題閱讀理解選擇題，評量學生對文章的理解程度，訓練五大閱讀技巧。

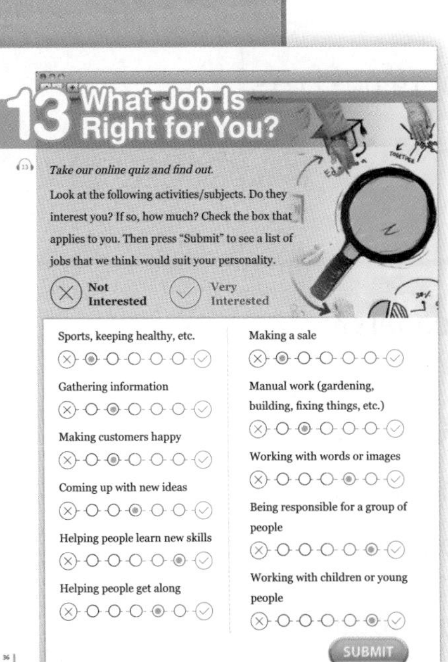

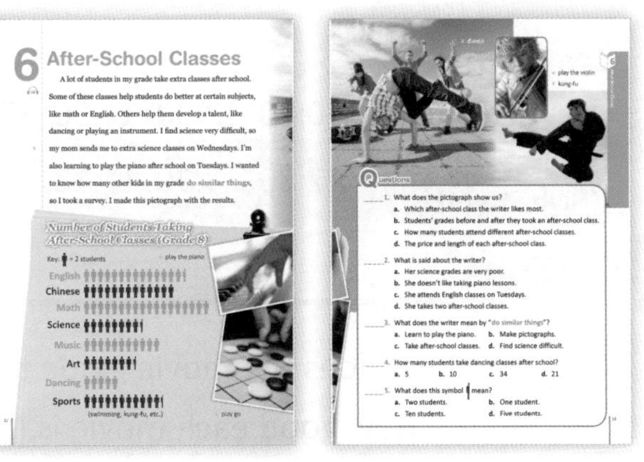

豐富多彩的圖表

運用大量彩色圖表與圖解，搭配文章輕鬆學習，以視覺輔助記憶，學習成效加倍。

1 A Day at the Movies

01

My friends and I want to go see a movie today. We picked up a newspaper at the convenience store. The movie times are at the back. Let's see what's showing today.

Movie Guide

A Good Day to Fight

Big Screen	10:10 12:40 14:40 17:10 19:10 21:40
Lights Out	09:30 12:20 14:35 19:15 23:25
LUX Cinema	10:00 12:15 13:15 14:35 16:50 17:50 19:05 20:05 21:20
New Theater	10:20 12:30 14:30 17:10
Showtime (High Street)	11:20 13:20 15:15 16:40 18:20 21:30 22:50
Showtime (Main Street)	11:20 13:40 15:50 18:10 20:20 22:40

Men of War

Big Screen	14:35 16:50 17:50
Lights Out	12:20 17:15

Last Look

New Theater	10:20 12:30 14:30 17:00 19:00 21:15
Showtime (High Street)	12:30 14:30 17:10 20:30 22:40

Questions

______ 1. What does the movie guide tell readers?

a. How good each movie is.

b. When and where the movies will play.

c. Who the main stars of each movie are.

d. How much each movie cost to make.

______ 2. Which movie is showing most often today?

a. *Men of War.*

b. *Ghost in the Dark.*

c. *A Good Day to Fight.*

d. *Space Race 3.*

« popcorn ≈ audience ≈ movie theater

The Future Is Now

Lights Out	10:00 12:15 13:15 14:35 19:10 21:15
LUX Cinema	11:20 13:40 15:50 18:10 20:20 22:40
New Theater	14:35 16:50 17:50 21:40

Space Race 3

Lights Out	12:20 14:50 17:30 19:10
LUX Cinema	13:45 17:50 19:30 21:15
New Theater	10:00 12:15 13:15 14:35 17:10 21:15
Showtime (High Street)	12:30 15:30 17:30 21:30 23:30
Showtime (Main Street)	12:20 14:10 17:15 20:40 22:10

Ghost in the Dark

Big Screen	12:00
LUX Cinema	13:30
New Theater	14:40
Showtime (Main Street)	10:00

» movie tickets

» convenience store

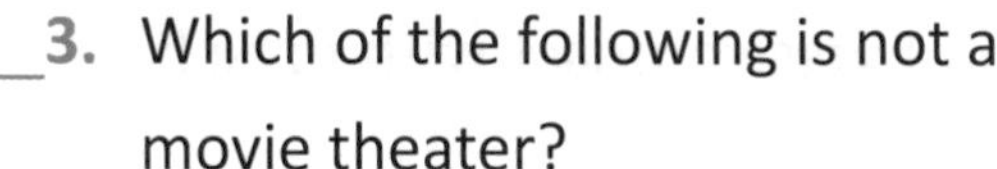

______ **3.** Which of the following is not a movie theater?

a. Last Look. **b.** Showtime.
c. Big Screen. **d.** Lights Out.

______ **4.** It's 12:30 p.m. When's the next showing of *The Future Is Now* ?

a. 1:15 p.m. **b.** 1:00 p.m. **c.** 2:35 p.m. **d.** 12:40 p.m.

______ **5.** What's the latest time my friends and I can see *Ghost in the Dark* today?

a. 1:30 p.m. **b.** 3:15 p.m. **c.** 4:40 p.m. **d.** 2:40 p.m.

2

02

What Makes a Good Friend?

Dina: I still can't believe Tara would date my ex-boyfriend so soon after we broke up.

Lisa: I can. She's always been a selfish person who only cares about herself. To be honest, I don't understand why you are friends with her. She doesn't care about your happiness at all.

Dina: Wow. You sound just like my mother. She's always telling me that good friends care about your happiness as much as their own.

Lisa: Well, she's right. Also, **you two really don't have anything in common**. You're a good student who wants to be successful . . .

Dina: . . . and she would rather spend her time shopping and thinking about boys.

Lisa: Remember that time she convinced you to help her find the perfect new dress when you should have been studying?

Dina: I sure do. I failed that test and I was so upset with myself.

Lisa: See? She doesn't care about your needs in the least. If I were you, I would end the friendship.

Dina: You're right. It's not a healthy friendship. I need more people like you in my life. Thanks for being honest.

Lisa: That's what good friends do!

^ friendship

Questions

____ 1. What could be another title for this reading?
- **a.** How to Find True Happiness
- **b.** What Is a Healthy Friendship?
- **c.** Why Are People So Selfish?
- **d.** Studying for Success

____ 2. Why does Dina need more people like Lisa in her life?
- **a.** Lisa likes helping people study.
- **b.** Dina doesn't have many friends.
- **c.** It's important to have selfish friends.
- **d.** Lisa cares about Dina's happiness.

____ 3. What does "**you two really don't have anything in common**" mean in this reading?
- **a.** Tara and Dina don't really like each other.
- **b.** Tara and Dina don't live in the same area.
- **c.** Tara and Dina have different interests.
- **d.** Tara and Dina have different sets of friends.

____ 4. Which two people have told Dina that Tara is selfish?
- **a.** Tara and Dina's other friend.
- **b.** Lisa and Tara.
- **c.** Tara and Dina's mom.
- **d.** Dina's mom and Lisa.

____ 5. Why was Dina upset with herself?
- **a.** She broke up with her boyfriend.
- **b.** She didn't prepare for a test.
- **c.** She couldn't find the perfect dress.
- **d.** She didn't listen to her mother.

3 English Forum

03

Maria132

At 14:15, Maria132 wrote:

Hi everyone,

My English teacher gave me this question for homework, but I don't know the answer. Can someone help me?

On Mondays, I'm usually at work **until/since** 7 p.m.

Which one is correct? Please help!

Thanks. **Maria**

RedHarry67

At 14:30, RedHarry67 replied:

The correct answer is **until**. Use **since** to say when something **that's still happening now** began (e.g., *I'm at work now. I've been working **since** 7 a.m.*).

Use **until** to say when something ends (**e.g.**, *I start work at 7 a.m., and I don't finish **until** 7 p.m.*).

I hope that helps! **Harry**

KipJones21

At 14:42, KipJones21 replied:

You should be able to work out the answer from the tense of the sentence.

With **since**, we usually use the present perfect (have/has + past participle) or present perfect continuous (have/has been + -ing). If the sentence was "I have been at work **until/since** 7 p.m.," then the right answer would be **since**. But in your sentence you're talking about regular action using the simple present tense ("I'm usually at work . . ."), so **since** isn't possible. **Kip**

Maria132

At 14:50, Maria132 replied:

Thanks Kip and Harry for your help!

It's much clearer now! :)

Questions

_____ 1. What is Maria trying to find?

- **a.** A person with whom she can practice her English.
- **b.** Someone to teach her business English.
- **c.** The answer to an English grammar question.
- **d.** A job in an English school.

_____ 2. What does Kip say about "**since**" ?

- **a.** It's usually used with the present perfect tense.
- **b.** It's used to talk about regular action.
- **c.** It's used to say when something ends.
- **d.** It's used with the simple present tense.

_____ 3. What does Maria mean when she says, "**It's much clearer now**"?

- **a.** She's confused.
- **b.** She needs time to think.
- **c.** She wants to start over.
- **d.** She understands.

_____ 4. Which of these is probably true about Maria?

- **a.** She can speak English at an advanced level.
- **b.** Harry is her English teacher.
- **c.** English is not her first language.
- **d.** They don't teach English at her school.

_____ 5. What does "**e.g.**" most likely mean?

- **a.** And others.
- **b.** For example.
- **c.** In other words.
- **d.** Compare.

4 Get Home Safe

04

Sue

Hi, Mom! Can I go to Julie's house after school? She got a new hamster and I want to see it.

Mom

Not today, my dear. I don't want you walking home in the dark.

Sue

Don't be so **old school**, Mom. I can walk home in the dark.

Mom

Not a chance!

Sue

But Mindy's parents let her stay out until 9 p.m.

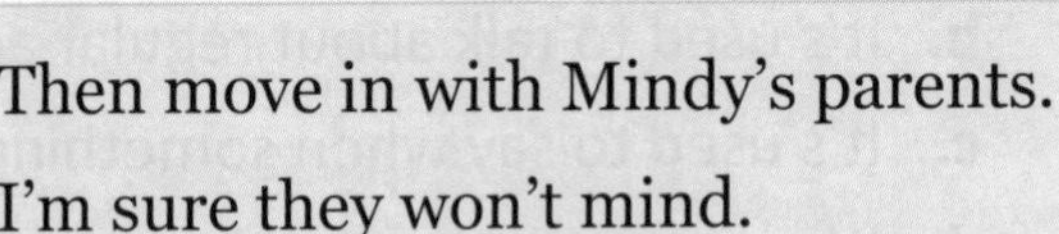
Then move in with Mindy's parents. I'm sure they won't mind.

Mom

Sue

Please, just this once! I promise I'll do the dishes for a week.

do the dishes

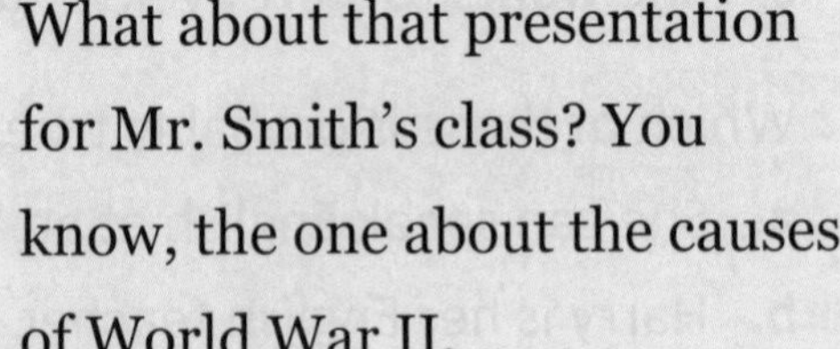
What about that presentation for Mr. Smith's class? You know, the one about the causes of World War II.

Mom

Sue

I **wrapped that up** two weeks ago.

presentation

All right, then. You can stay at Julie's house until 7 p.m. and have a late dinner.

Hurray! My evening is saved.

Since I'm so **old school**, you probably know what I'm going to say next, right?

You'll say something like "Come right home and don't talk to any strangers, my dear."

Couldn't have said it better myself.

Questions

_____ **1.** What point is the mother in this conversation trying to make?

a. Finish your homework. **b.** Don't come home until 9 p.m.
c. Don't stay out too late. **d.** Move to Mindy's house.

_____ **2.** Why does Sue want to go to Julie's house?

a. To work on her homework.
b. To hang out with Julie and Mindy.
c. To practice her presentation.
d. To see Julie's new pet.

_____ **3.** What does Sue mean when she calls her Mom "**old school**"?

a. Her mom is too old. **b.** Her mom is old-fashioned.
c. Her mom is really nice. **d.** Her mom is really smart.

_____ **4.** What class does Mr. Smith likely teach?

a. Math. **b.** Science. **c.** History. **d.** Gym.

_____ **5.** What does Sue mean when she says that she "**wrapped that up**"?

a. She hasn't started it. **b.** She gave up on it.
c. She finished it. **d.** She hasn't heard of it.

05

5 Jane's Notebook

» coach

Sept. 1

I found another note in my desk today. It was signed "from your secret admirer." I really hope it's not Jim who's writing these.

Sept. 5

I am **done with training**. I don't care if there will be two big events in November. How can my coach expect me to do 10 kilometers every two days? Not at all surprising since the man is a robot. I shouldn't expect him to know how we humans feel pain.

Sept. 7

Jim finally worked up the courage to talk to me after class. He asked if I could add him as a friend on Facebook. I told him I didn't have a Facebook account. Judging by the look on his face, I don't think he believed me.

Facebook account

Sept. 13

Almost a week without any new notes. Looks like my "secret admirer" finally **got the picture**.

Sept. 15

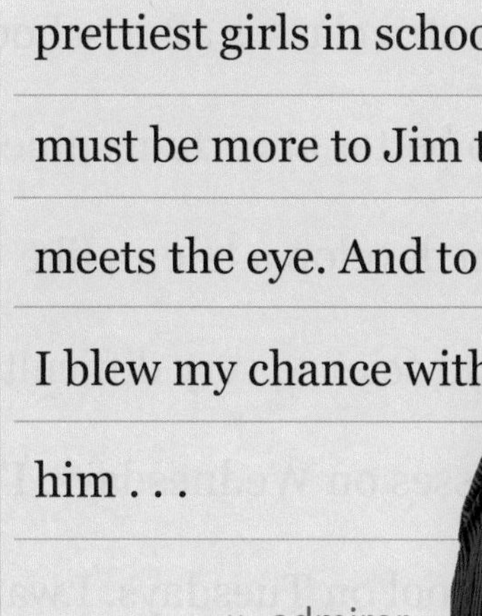

Jim is going out with Sarah! How did this happen? She's one of the prettiest girls in school. There must be more to Jim than meets the eye. And to think I blew my chance with him . . .

» admirer

Questions

_____ 1. What is this reading about?
- a. Jane's Facebook.
- b. Jane's life.
- c. Jane's friends.
- d. Jane's training.

_____ 2. Who is Jane's secret admirer?
- a. Her coach.
- b. Jim.
- c. Sarah.
- d. We don't know.

_____ 3. What does it mean that Jane is "**done with training**"?
- a. She doesn't know how to train.
- b. She doesn't want to train anymore.
- c. She has been training for a short time.
- d. She is training very well.

_____ 4. What is Jane likely training for?
- a. Running events.
- b. The baseball team.
- c. Math events.
- d. Chess events.

_____ 5. What does it mean to "**get the picture**"?
- a. To understand something.
- b. To paint.
- c. To buy a piece of art.
- d. To not like someone.

6 After-School Classes

A lot of students in my grade take extra classes after school. Some of these classes help students do better at certain subjects, like math or English. Others help them develop a talent, like dancing or playing an instrument. I find science very difficult, so my mom sends me to extra science classes on Wednesdays. I'm also learning to play the piano after school on Tuesdays. I wanted to know how many other kids in my grade **do similar things**, so I took a survey. I made this pictograph with the results.

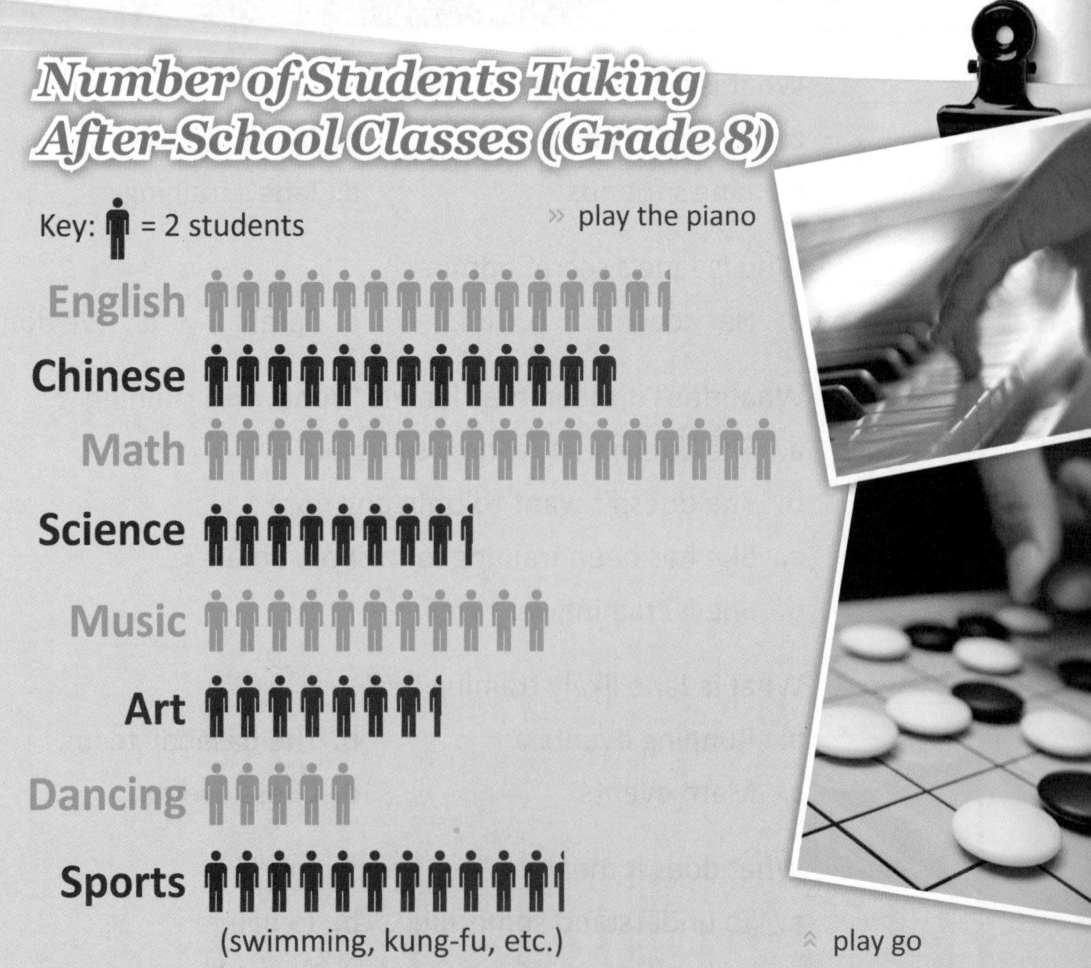

Questions

_____ 1. What does the pictograph show us?

a. Which after-school class the writer likes most.

b. Students' grades before and after they took an after-school class.

c. How many students attend different after-school classes.

d. The price and length of each after-school class.

_____ 2. What is said about the writer?

a. Her science grades are very poor.

b. She doesn't like taking piano lessons.

c. She attends English classes on Tuesdays.

d. She takes two after-school classes.

_____ 3. What does the writer mean by "**do similar things**"?

a. Learn to play the piano. b. Make pictographs.

c. Take after-school classes. d. Find science difficult.

_____ 4. How many students take dancing classes after school?

a. 5 b. 10 c. 34 d. 21

_____ 5. What does this symbol mean?

a. Two students. b. One student.

c. Ten students. d. Five students.

07

7 Love and Divorce

Mavis

Dear Mavis,

I'm 15 years old and I'm worried that my parents are going to get a divorce. It's not the arguing; they've been doing that for as long as I can remember. It's their total indifference that's **getting to me**. Sometimes we sit down for dinner and nobody says a word for the entire meal. It's like they're not even married. Neither of them seems to care what the other one thinks or feels. This isn't what you'd call normal, is it? Thanks for listening to my problem. I'm a longtime reader and a big fan.

John

divorce

Questions

_____ **1.** What is this reading trying to say?

- **a.** John's parents don't love him.
- **b.** Dinner is an important meal.
- **c.** John's parents are angry.
- **d.** Marriage problems is hard on children.

_____ **2.** Which of the following statements is not true?

- **a.** John is a teenager.
- **b.** John's parents fight a lot.
- **c.** Mavis is John's mother.
- **d.** No one speaks at dinner time.

Dear John,

It sounds like your family is going through a difficult time. I can't say whether your parents will get a divorce or not. However, you must not forget that they still love you no matter what happens. When we're young, we think that our parents always know what they're doing. Well, they don't always know. Your mom and dad are probably confused and don't know what to do next. This can make them **act out** in strange ways.

I hope this helps.

Mavis

_____ **3.** What does it mean when people "**act out**"?

a. They are happy. **b.** They are behaving badly.

c. They are eating a meal. **d.** They are confused.

_____ **4.** What kind of job does Mavis likely have?

a. She is a police officer. **b.** She is a writer for a magazine.

c. She is a lawyer. **d.** She is a firefighter.

_____ **5.** What does it mean when John says it's "**getting to me**"?

a. It makes him angry. **b.** It confuses him.

c. It makes him tired. **d.** He doesn't care about it.

8 How Low Is Enough?

The smallest amount that a worker can be paid is called the minimum wage. It's an important number because it affects the quality of life of millions of workers around the world.

Every country has a different minimum wage. Politicians use the cost of living to set it. They ask, "How much does a worker need to **make ends meet**?" The problem is that the situation is always changing. Sometimes the costs of food, gas, and rent go up but the minimum wage stays the same. This can make it hard on workers.

Politicians don't like raising the minimum wage because they feel it hurts businesses, which need to pay more for their workers. However, many disagree with this. They say that a higher minimum wage puts more money in everyone's pocket. That means people spend more, and the economy improves as a result.

≈ wage

» workers

Minimum Monthly Wage in Taiwan

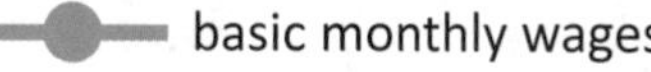

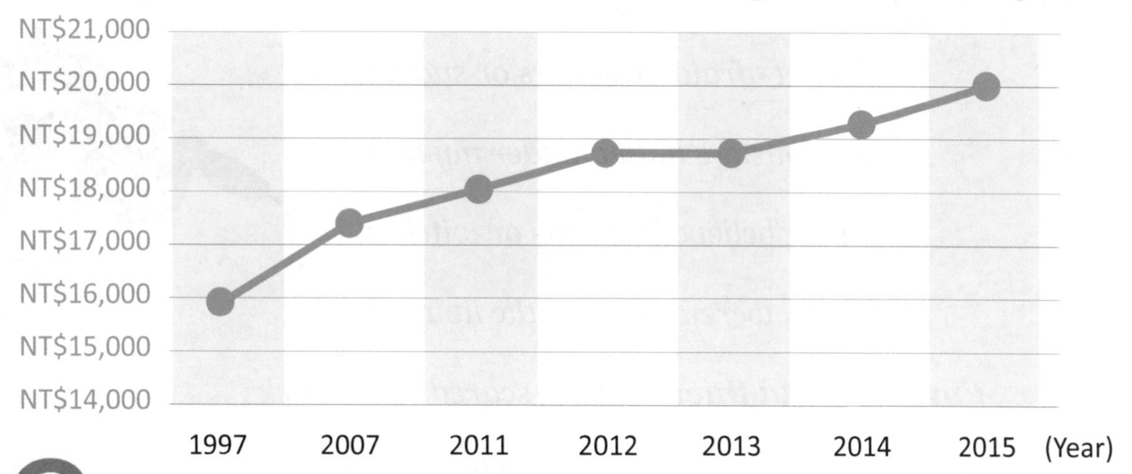

Questions

_____ **1.** What is the main idea of this reading?

a. The minimum wage should not be changed.
b. The minimum wage can hurt businesses.
c. The minimum wage is important for workers.
d. The minimum wage is set by politicians.

_____ **2.** What is one of the problems with the minimum wage?

a. It's always too high.
b. It doesn't keep up with the costs of gas and rent.
c. It changes too much.
d. It's welcomed by most workers.

» politician

_____ **3.** What does "**make ends meet**" mean?

a. Meet a new friend. **b.** Make a new piece of clothing.
c. Hold a meeting. **d.** Make enough money to live.

_____ **4.** Which year had the lowest monthly minimum wage?

a. 1997 **b.** 2007 **c.** 2011 **d.** 2012

_____ **5.** Which of the following is the monthly minimum wage in 2015?

a. NT$19,872 **b.** NT$20,000 **c.** NT$18,654 **d.** NT$17,000

9 My Greatest Fear

09

I'm not afraid of spiders or snakes,
or monsters hiding under my bed.
I don't believe in ghosts or witches,
vampires, werewolves, or the living dead.
I'm a natural flyer*; I'm not scared of the dark.*
Rats I find adorable; I'd even swim with sharks.
So what am I scared of?
Well, there's this one dream that I have,
night after night after night,
that one morning I wake up to find
there's not a soul in sight*—nobody but me.*

Questions

_____ **1.** What is the writer trying to do in the poem?

a. Show off how brave she is.
b. Talk about her hopes and dreams.
c. Show how independent she is.
d. Figure out what she's scared of.

_____ **2.** Which of these happens at the end of the writer's dream?

a. She makes lots of new friends.
b. She flies off into space.
c. She goes crazy.
d. She hears a scary story.

« werewolf

Empty streets and houses; nobody on TV.
And I think, maybe they all just left me to go to another world,
Let's just leave her here, *they thought.*
Such an irritating girl.
I have to talk to myself, which is fine at first.
But then after a while there's nothing worse
than hearing the same stories, over and over again,
and no one there to make new stories with . . .
In the end I go mad! Just me, there on my own.
You know, the thing I might be most scared of is . . .

» vampire

» the living dead

______**3.** What does "**there's not a soul in sight**" mean?

a. There's nobody around. **b.** Somebody died nearby.
c. The writer can't see. **d.** Everyone's in a bad mood.

______**4.** What is the writer's greatest fear?

a. Breaking a bone. **b.** Never going home.
c. Being all alone. **d.** Getting hit with a stone.

______**5.** What does the writer mean by "**I'm a natural flyer**"?

a. She's really scared of flying. **b.** She's never flown before.
c. She wants to learn how to fly. **d.** She's not scared of flying.

10 Assembly Instructions

From: service@gomail.com

To: Cindy@xyzmail.com

Subject: Re: Assembly Instructions

Dear Cindy,

Don't worry! You're not the first person who has had a hard time putting together our *Primo* model. I am happy to **walk you through** the process. Here are step-by-step instructions:

≈ board

1) Collect what you'll need to put it together. You should have four leg pieces, four metal braces, the top and bottom boards, four plastic feet, and 16 screws.
2) Prepare the leg pieces by putting a plastic foot on each one.
3) Find the bottom side of the top board. It is the one with holes for the screws. Now screw in the metal braces using four screws per brace.
4) Take the four legs and slide them into the metal braces. Now it can stand up on its own with the four plastic feet on the ground.
5) Take the bottom board and slide it in under the top board, so it is held in place by the four legs.

If you want to get the most from your *Primo*, we suggest painting the top board. This will help protect it from the wear and tear of years of family dinners.

≈ instruction manual

≈ nuts

≈ screws

≈ screwdriver

Questions

_______ **1.** What is this reading about?

- **a.** Putting together the *Primo*.
- **b.** Preparing the leg pieces.
- **c.** Painting the top board.
- **d.** Protecting from wear and tear.

_______ **2.** Which of the following is not a part of the *Primo*?

- **a.** The four leg pieces.
- **b.** The top board.
- **c.** The shelf.
- **d.** The bottom board.

_______ **3.** What does "**walk you through**" mean in the reading ?

- **a.** To go to Cindy's house.
- **b.** To give slow, careful instructions.
- **c.** To give Cindy a picture of the *Primo*.
- **d.** To build the *Primo* for Cindy.

_______ **4.** The *Primo* is most likely what type of furniture?

- **a.** A chair.
- **b.** A shelf.
- **c.** A television stand.
- **d.** A table.

_______ **5.** Who is likely replying to Cindy in this letter?

- **a.** Her lawyer.
- **b.** Her customer.
- **c.** Customer support.
- **d.** A close friend.

11 She's Out of This World

11

I've been **seeing** this girl for a while now;
Thought she was the one for me.
But lately I've noticed some strange things.
Maybe you'll agree.

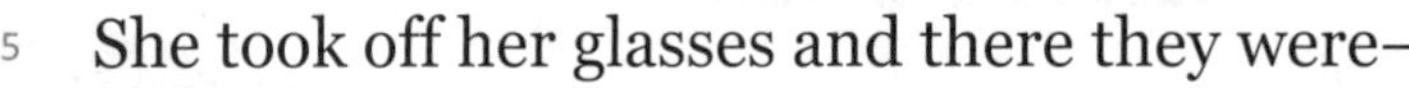

She took off her glasses and there they were—
Two big silver eyes.
And her hair isn't real; it comes off.
Boy, that was **some** surprise.
There's something not right about her—
Her legs are covered in purple fur . . .

» UFO

» whisper

Questions

_____ **1.** What is the singer trying to say in the song?

a. His girlfriend is really cute.
b. His girlfriend is not from this planet.
c. His girlfriend has a cool cell phone.
d. His girlfriend looks different from other girls.

_____ **2.** Which of these is not said about the singer's girlfriend?

a. She has a strange name.
b. Her ears are a strange shape.
c. Her eyes are a strange color.
d. Her skin feels strange to the touch.

_____ **3.** What does "**seeing**" mean here?

a. Dating. **b.** Visiting. **c.** Considering. **d.** Viewing.

[Chorus]
My girlfriend is not normal.
She's really cute, but I think she's an alien.
My mom thinks it's just a teenage thing.
But her skin is green. Her skin is green . . .

aliens

I caught her whispering on a strange-looking cell phone,
Speaking in a language that I didn't know.
I think that she might have been talking
With someone far away on a UFO.

fur

There's something not right about her—
She has really pointy ears . . .
[Chorus]
There's something not right about her—Her full name is Zxyzxyblr.
[Chorus]

______ **4.** Which of the following sentences uses "**some**" in the same sense as the song does?

- **a.** There were some people here earlier looking for you.
- **b.** Some party, Joe. I won't forget that in a hurry!
- **c.** I saw some guy stealing Jake's bag.
- **d.** I like some rock music, but not a lot.

______ **5.** Lots of songs have deeper meanings. What might the deeper meaning of this song be?

- **a.** Boys like girls who dress and act strangely.
- **b.** Boys should always listen to their mothers.
- **c.** For boys, girls can be very difficult to understand.
- **d.** It's a bad idea for teenagers to fall in love.

12 Teatime for Class 3B

12

There's kind of a tradition in my class at school. Every lunchtime, we all go out to buy some tea at one of the nearby teashops. Until recently, there were only two tea shops, Jill's Tea Shop and Tasty Tea. But at the end of April, I heard that a new tea shop called Tea 4 U would be opening at the beginning of May. I was curious—how would this new competition affect the other shops? And how would my classmates decide where to go for their tea? Would they stay **loyal** to their regular tea shop, or would they want to try something new? So, every lunchtime for the whole of May, I asked all of them where they had gotten their tea from, and I made this area graph to show the results.

green tea

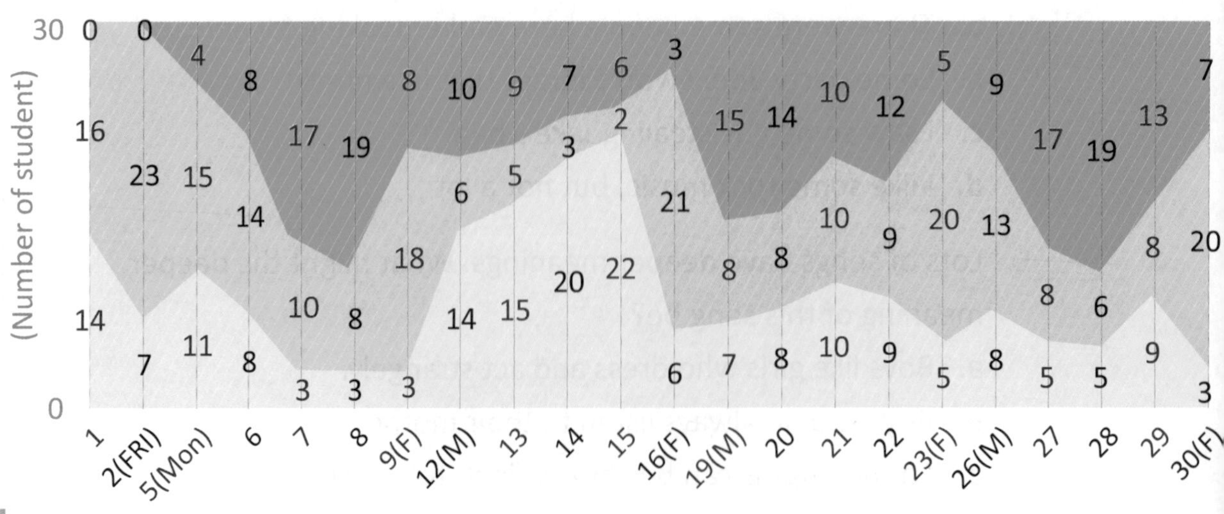

« black tea

« fruit tea

« herbal tea

Questions

_____ 1. What does the graph show?

- **a.** Which type of tea the students bought each day.
- **b.** What the students thought of the tea they bought.
- **c.** At which shop students bought their tea each day.
- **d.** How much the tea at each shop costs.

_____ 2. What happened to make the writer want to create this graph?

- **a.** One of the nearby tea shops closed down.
- **b.** A new tea shop opened near his school.
- **c.** His classmates began buying tea at lunchtime.
- **d.** The school began serving tea at lunchtime.

_____ 3. What does it mean to be "**loyal**"?

- **a.** Supporting someone always.
- **b.** Following the crowd.
- **c.** Happily trying new things.
- **d.** Not taking part at all.

_____ 4. On one day each week, Tasty Tea has a buy-one-get-one-free offer on tea. What day do you think that is?

- **a.** Monday.
- **b.** Friday.
- **c.** Wednesday.
- **d.** Thursday.

_____ 5. One Monday, this notice was posted outside the school. On what date was it most likely posted?

- **a.** May 1.
- **b.** May 25.
- **c.** May 11.
- **d.** May 18.

Jill's Tea Shop

Attention All Students!
40% off *any tea drink this week*
for anyone
wearing a school uniform.
Come on down
and enjoy some tea!

13 What Job Is Right for You?

13

Take our online quiz and find out.

Look at the following activities/subjects. Do they interest you? If so, how much? Check the box that applies to you. Then press "Submit" to see a list of jobs that we think would suit your personality.

Not Interested

Very Interested

Sports, keeping healthy, etc.

Gathering information

Making customers happy

Coming up with new ideas

Helping people learn new skills

Helping people get along

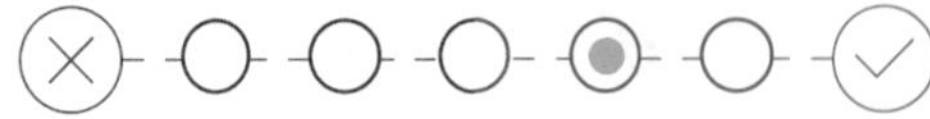

Making a sale

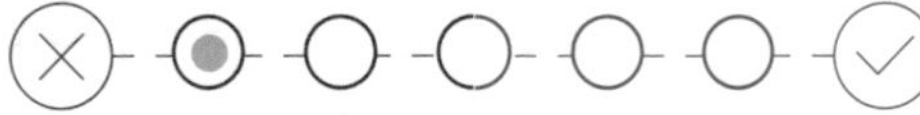

Manual work (gardening, building, fixing things, etc.)

Working with words or images

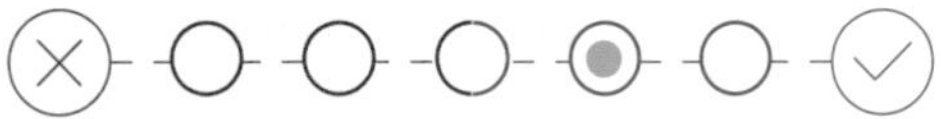

Being responsible for a group of people

Working with children or young people

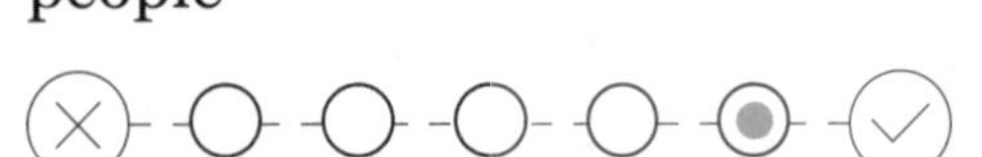

SUBMIT

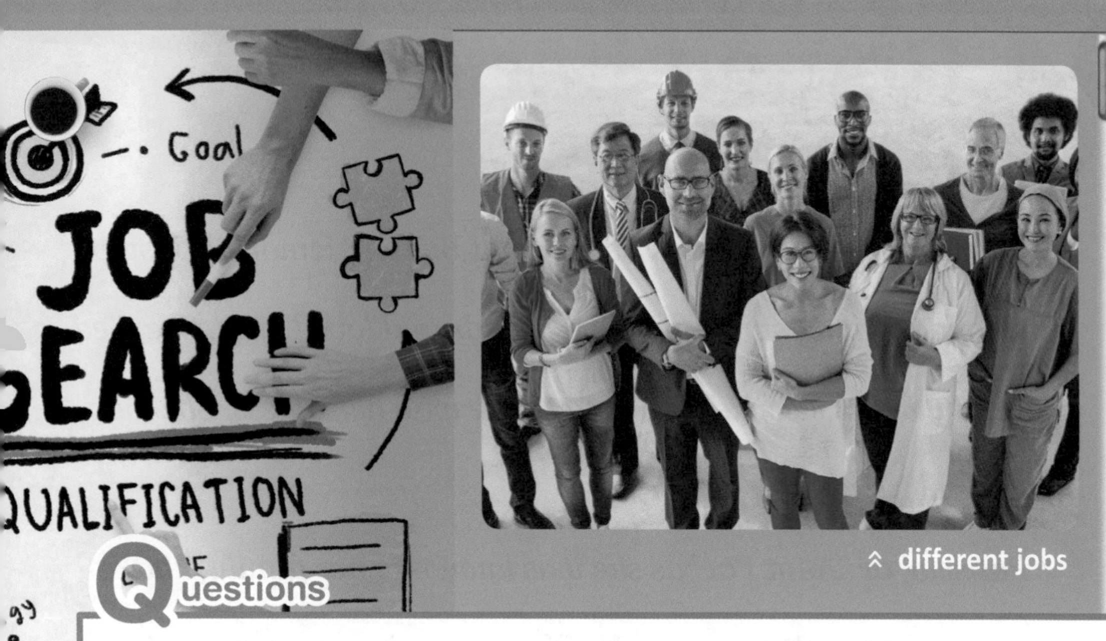

⌃ different jobs

Questions

_____ 1. What can you find out by taking this quiz?
- **a.** How much money you should be earning.
- **b.** What type of person you are.
- **c.** How smart you are.
- **d.** Which type of work suits you.

_____ 2. How does the person who took the quiz feel about sports?
- **a.** So-so.
- **b.** Very interested.
- **c.** Not interested at all.
- **d.** Quite interested.

_____ 3. What does "**manual work**" mean?
- **a.** Working with your hands.
- **b.** Working in an office.
- **c.** Working with computers.
- **d.** Working with animals.

_____ 4. What can we guess about the person who took this quiz?
- **a.** He or she wants to get more education.
- **b.** He or she is unsure about his or her future.
- **c.** He or she doesn't like his or her boss.
- **d.** He or she just found a new job.

_____ 5. Look at the answers the person gave. What result did he or she most likely get?
- **a.** Salesman.
- **b.** Banker.
- **c.** Teacher.
- **d.** Mechanic.

14 Remembering Aunt Pat

14

Patricia Sarah Smith passed away at Bolton Memorial Hospital late Monday night, surrounded by friends and loved ones. She died peacefully in her sleep after a long battle with her illness. She was 75 years old.

Patricia, or "Aunt Pat" as she was known to her family, had a very eventful life. She came to Halifax when she was just a baby. Anyone who knew her growing up will tell you the same thing: Patricia was ***no stranger*** *to mischief. She never liked playing with dolls or throwing tea parties. Climbing trees and playing baseball were more her style.*

She calmed down when Arthur entered her life. He was devoted to Pat, and even insisted on carrying her books at school. After 40 years of marriage and three children, their love burned as brightly as on the first day they met. Here were two ***soul mates*** *in every sense of the term.*

We should not mourn her passing, though she will be missed. She had a long life full of love and happiness, and for that we should celebrate.

» doll

Questions

_____ **1.** What is this reading about?

a. Aunt Pat's illness.
b. Aunt Pat's friends.
c. Aunt Pat's school.
d. Aunt Pat's life.

_____ **2.** Which of the following is not true about Aunt Pat?

a. She had children.
b. She was 40 years old.
c. She was married.
d. She died in a hospital.

_____ **3.** What does it mean to be "**no stranger**" to something?

a. You do it a lot.
b. You don't know about it.
c. You're scared of it.
d. You have done it once before.

_____ **4.** Which of the following is probably something Aunt Pat liked to do when she was young?

a. Go shopping for a dress.
b. Make cookies.
c. Go for a bike ride.
d. Clean the house.

_____ **5.** What does it mean if two people are "**soul mates**"?

a. They look the same.
b. They are meant to be together.
c. They go to the same school.
d. They grew up in the same place.

15 Let's Play Ball!

15

» National League logo

I love baseball. It's my favorite sport. Taiwan's professional baseball league (the CPBL) only has four teams competing in it. That's not many compared to the US's National Baseball League, which has 38 teams playing in it. **Still**, each team plays 120 games a year, so keeping track of all the wins (W), ties (T), and losses (L) can be tough. That's why, during the season, the scores for each team are entered into a table. These are the league tables at the end of this year's season.

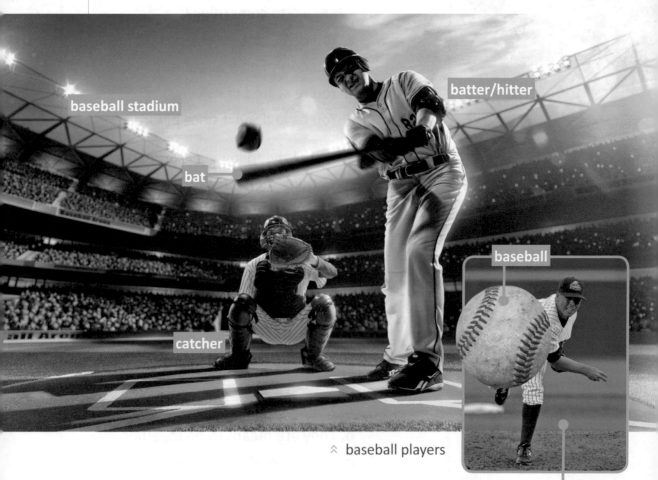

^ baseball players

« baseball field

Rank	Team	W-T-L	Lamigo Monkeys	Uni-President Lions	EDA Rhinos	Brother Elephants
1	Lamigo Monkeys	66-3-51	-	20-2-18	20-0-20	26-1-13
2	Uni-President Lions	58-7-55	18-2-20	-	21-2-17	19-3-18
3	EDA Rhinos	58-2-60	20-0-20	17-2-21	-	21-0-19
4	Brother Elephants	50-4-66	13-1-26	18-3-19	19-0-21	-

*These scores are from the 2014 CPBL season results.

Questions

_____ 1. What does the table show?

a. The baseball results for this season.

b. Ticket prices for a baseball game.

c. The writer's favorite baseball teams in order.

d. The times and places of this season's games.

_____ 2. How many teams play in the CPBL?

a. 38 b. 120 c. 4 d. 2

_____ 3. Which of these words could you use in place of "**Still**" in the article?

a. Even. b. Now. c. However. d. Therefore.

_____ 4. Which team had the most losses this season?

a. The EDA Rhinos. b. The Brother Elephants.

c. The Lamigo Monkeys. d. The Uni-President Lions.

_____ 5. How many games did the EDA Rhinos win against the Uni-President Lions this season?

a. 17 b. 2 c. 21 d. 58

16

Apple Yahoo! Google Maps YouTube Wikipedia News (1002) Popular

What's a Berry?

2015/08/26

Here's something I'll bet you didn't know: strawberries aren't berries. Neither are raspberries, nor blackberries. All of these so-called berries are complex fruits, meaning they develop from flowers with many ovaries. A *true* berry, however, is a **simple** fruit, developing from a flower with only one ovary.

The ovary is the part of a flower which grows into a fruit after pollination. Some flowers have one ovary, while others have more. To be a berry, a fruit must be formed from a flower with only one ovary. This means that fruits such as grapes, bananas, tomatoes, and even watermelons are berries, while many things we *call* berries are not. In fact, the tiny "seeds" you see on the outside of a strawberry aren't seeds at all. Each is really an ovary from the original flower, with a seed inside. That's too many ovaries to count!

Just how people started calling complex fruits berries, and true berries other things, is a mystery. Even if we keep on making **that mistake**, though, at least now we'll know what we're really buying at the market.

Parts of a Flower

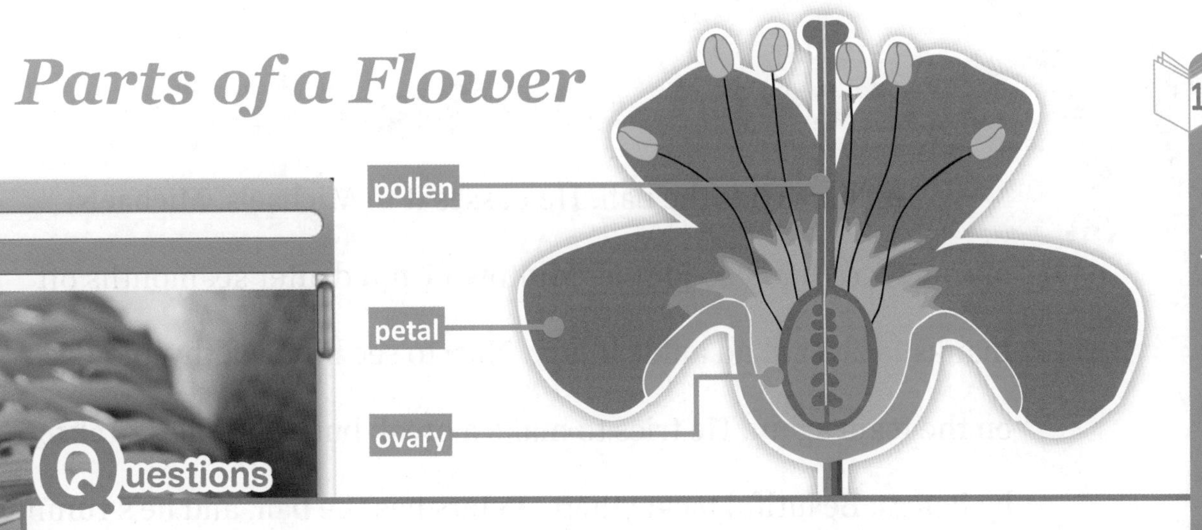

Questions

_____1. What could be another title for this reading?

a. How to Grow Strawberries in Your Home Garden.
b. Facts about Flowers.
c. Berries That Aren't Berries.
d. Shopping for Fruit at the Market.

_____2. Which of these fruits is a berry?

a. A raspberry. b. A blackberry.
c. A strawberry. d. A tomato.

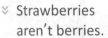

Strawberries aren't berries.

_____3. What does "**that mistake**" mean?

a. Using incorrect names for fruits.
b. Buying the wrong fruit at the market.
c. Counting the ovaries on a strawberry.
d. Trying to make fruit from flowers.

berries

_____4. What does "**simple**" mean as used in this reading?

a. Easy to understand. b. Not smart.
c. Singular. d. Multiple.

_____5. Which of the following statements is most likely true?

a. Everyone knows that strawberries aren't really berries.
b. Most people don't know that strawberries aren't really berries.
c. Only the writer knows that strawberries aren't really berries.
d. The writer doesn't know that strawberries aren't really berries.

17 Soccer Commentary

. . . Williams has the ball. He passes it to Michaels. Michaels, of course, recently re-joining Midtown United after six months off thanks to a very bad ankle injury. Nice to see him healthy and back on the team again. He tries to make a break but—oh!—he's **tackled** by Peters. Beautiful tackle there. Peters has the ball, and he's running now, past Daniels. Gray tries to tackle, but Peters is through! He's beaten both defenders. And now there's no one between **him** and the goalkeeper. Peters shoots! He

goalkeeper

shoot

Questions

______ 1. Which of the following does the speaker not talk about?

- **a.** What's going on in the match.
- **b.** The health of one of the players.
- **c.** Who he thinks will win the match.
- **d.** The best player of the match.

______ 2. What's the score at the end of the reading?

- **a.** Bringham City 2, Midtown United 1.
- **b.** Bringham City 1, Midtown United 2.
- **c.** Bringham City 1, Midtown United 1.
- **d.** Bringham City 0, Midtown United 1.

scores! Goal! Goal for Bringham City! That puts Bringham in the lead. It's 2–1 with three minutes left on the clock. I think Bringham City has the match. The way Midtown United has been playing in the second half, I don't think they'll be able to score another goal. Bringham City's defense has just been too strong. That one goal United managed late in the first half was really the high point of their game. Since then, they've been pretty much on the back foot the entire time. But we'll see how things go in these closing minutes . . .

⌃ score

_____ **3.** Who is "**him**"?

a. Peters. **b.** Michaels. **c.** Gray. **d.** The goalkeeper.

_____ **4.** What can we guess about Midtown's game?

a. They played better in the second half than in the first.
b. They played worse than Bringham city in both halves.
c. They played better in the first half than in the second.
d. They played better than Bringham city in both halves.

_____ **5.** In soccer, if you "**tackle**" someone, what do you do?

a. You take the ball from him. **b.** You kick the ball to him.
c. You throw the ball to him. **d.** You hurt him on purpose.

18 Magic Trick: Video Tutorial 18

» coin

Welcome, everyone, once again to Mike's Magic Class. Today I'm going to show you how to perform the coin-through-solid-glass trick.

First, the trick.

In my left hand I'm holding a small glass bowl, and in my right hand I have a coin. I place the coin in the palm of my right hand. Now I'm going to hit my palm against the bottom of the bowl once, . . . twice, . . . three times. And presto! The coin has passed through the bottom of the bowl and is now inside it.

Here's the **explanation**.

First, make sure you hold the bowl at the top between your thumb and middle finger, like this. Then, after you hit the bowl with your palm for the second time, secretly move the coin from your palm to your fingertips, like this. Then, when you hit the bottom of the bowl with your palm, the coin will jump from your fingertips, bounce off your left hand and fall into the bowl from above. But it will look like it passed through the bottom of the bowl.

Remember, everyone, **practice makes perfect**, so don't worry if you can't do it right away. And I'll see you guys next time!

Questions

_____1. What do you learn from this video?

a. The history of magic tricks.

b. The secret behind a magic trick.

c. Where and when you can see Mike perform.

d. Why coins are good for use in magic tricks.

_____2. Which of the following describes the magic effect shown in the video?

a. A coin seems to pass through glass.

b. A coin jumps from one hand to the other.

c. A bowl is broken in half and put back together again.

d. A pile of coins appears in an empty bowl.

_____3. What does an "**explanation**" do?

a. It makes something more fun.

b. It makes something harder to understand.

c. It makes something clear.

d. It makes something correct.

_____4. What is likely true about Mike?

a. This is his first-ever video.

b. He posts similar videos regularly.

c. He's a high school teacher.

d. He doesn't really like magic.

_____5. What does "**practice makes perfect**" mean?

a. If you can't do something well the first time, you should quit.

b. Some things are so difficult that they're impossible to do well.

c. You have to do something many times before you can do it well.

d. Some things are so easy that you can do them without trying.

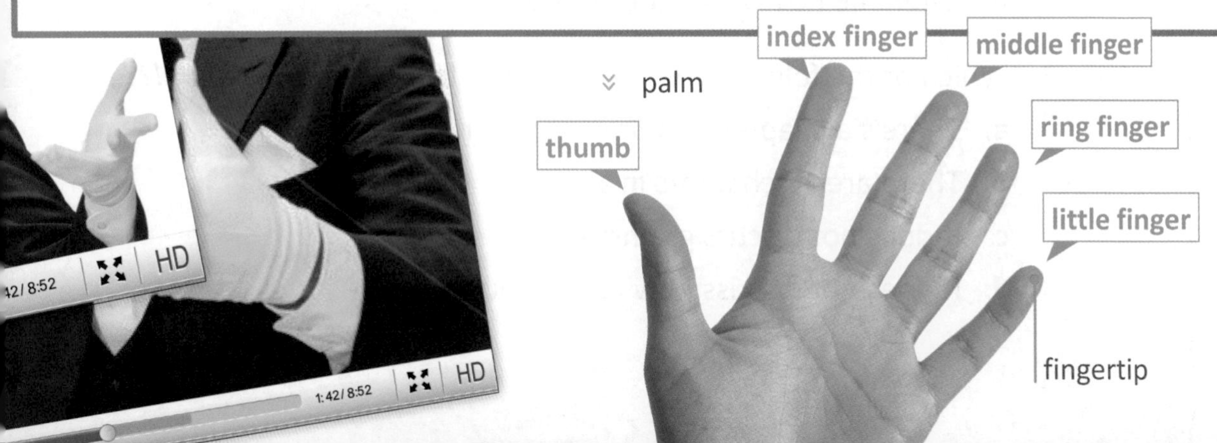

19 A Writer's Best Friend

19

Writing is a wonderful thing, but it doesn't come easy. Mastering it takes time, hard work, and a bit of outside help. This is the interesting thing about writing. You can read hundreds of books on how to be a good writer. However, they won't necessarily help you. A better way to improve your skills is to read any book that you can get your hands on. That way you absorb different styles of writing and telling a story. And then there's the most important advice of all: sit down and get to work. The more you write, the easier it gets.

Canada's Gabrielle Roy once asked, "How could we know each other in the slightest if not for art?" She makes a **good point**. So pick up that pen and show the world what you're made of.

Questions

______ **1.** What is this reading trying to say?

- **a.** Reading helps us absorb different types of writing.
- **b.** Writing is more important than reading.
- **c.** Being a good writer takes a lot of hard work.
- **d.** Gabrielle Roy is a famous writer.

______ **2.** Which of the following is not true about the *Writer's Manual*?

- **a.** There's a chapter on business writing.
- **b.** There are 10 chapters in all.
- **c.** It does not discuss grammar.
- **d.** It does not discuss how to sell your book.

» Writing is a wonderful thing.

Writer's Manual

Table of Contents

Chapter 1	The Power of Good Writing
Chapter 2	Tools of the Trade
Chapter 3	The Right Workspace
Chapter 4	Grammar and Syntax
Chapter 5	What Famous People Have to Say on Writing
Chapter 6	The Importance of the Sentence
Chapter 7	Writing the Perfect Paper
Chapter 8	Writing a Good Story
Chapter 9	Writing Poetry
Chapter 10	Business Writing

» grammar

_____ **3.** What does it mean that Gabrielle Roy makes a "**good point**"?

a. She is a very good writer. **b.** She said something that's true.
c. She is a good person. **d.** She is curious about something.

_____ **4.** If someone wants to build the perfect office to write in, which chapter should he or she look at?

a. Chapter 1. **b.** Chapter 3. **c.** Chapter 7. **d.** Chapter 10.

_____ **5.** In what chapter might someone find how to write a business plan?

a. Chapter 9. **b.** Chapter 10. **c.** Chapter 8. **d.** Chapter 2.

20 Short Story Competition

We want your writing!

Think you can write a winning story? Enter the 17th Annual Newtown Library Short Story Competition for your chance to win $1,000. The three winning entries will also be published in the *Newtown Times*.

type

Prizes

1st Place: A check for $1000 and publication in the *Newtown Times.*

2nd Place: Publication in the *Newtown Times* and $300 in book tokens.

3rd Place: Publication in the *Newtown Times* and $150 in book tokens.

Questions

_____ **1.** What is the reading encouraging people to do?

a. Visit the library. **b.** Read the newspaper.
c. Write stories. **d.** Buy more books.

_____ **2.** I entered a story for the competition. It was 2,500 words long and typed on white paper, size A4. The font I used was Times New Roman. My story was sent back to me unread. Why?

a. It was too long. **b.** It should have been written by hand.
c. I used the wrong font. **d.** The paper was the wrong size.

_____ **3.** What does it mean to do something "**in person**"?

a. You ask a friend to do it for you.
b. You go somewhere and do it yourself.
c. You do it by mail.
d. You get a group of people to help you.

Google Maps YouTube Wikipedia News (1002) Popular

How to Enter

Send your entry by post to the Newtown Public Library, 45 High Street, Newtown, or come by and hand it in **in person**.

You can enter as many stories as you like!

- Please type your entry on white A4 paper. Use Times New Roman font, size 12. Handwritten entries will not be accepted.
- The word limit for each story is 2,000 words.
- Please also include your full name and contact information on the first page.

Your entry must be your own work and unpublished at the time of submission.

We look forward to reading your work!

» online newspaper

^ handwritten

______ **4.** What is true about the competition?

- **a.** If you write more than one story you will not win the prize.
- **b.** The more stories that are entered, the more the prize money will be.
- **c.** You can only enter a story if you are a published writer.
- **d.** There's no limit on the number of stories you can enter.

______ **5.** What does the phrase "**Your entry must be your own work**" mean?

- **a.** You must type up the story yourself.
- **b.** You can't ask anyone what he or she thinks about your story.
- **c.** You're not allowed to copy from other writers.
- **d.** You shouldn't enter a story if you don't have a job.

» black gold

21 Black Gold

Ever wonder why they call oil "black gold"? It's because it's so useful! We can use it to power our cars or keep our houses warm. It even shows up in household items like shampoo and toothpaste.

Given oil's usefulness, it's no surprise that governments are always **on edge** about how much it costs. On the surface, the price of oil is a simple calculation; it's determined by supply and demand. If there's too much of it, the price drops. If there isn't enough, the price goes up. But there's more to it than that. The price is also determined by what people think will happen. This means prices can skyrocket at the first hint of war in an oil-producing country.

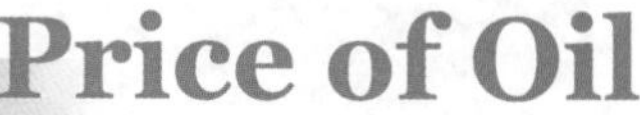

Price of Oil

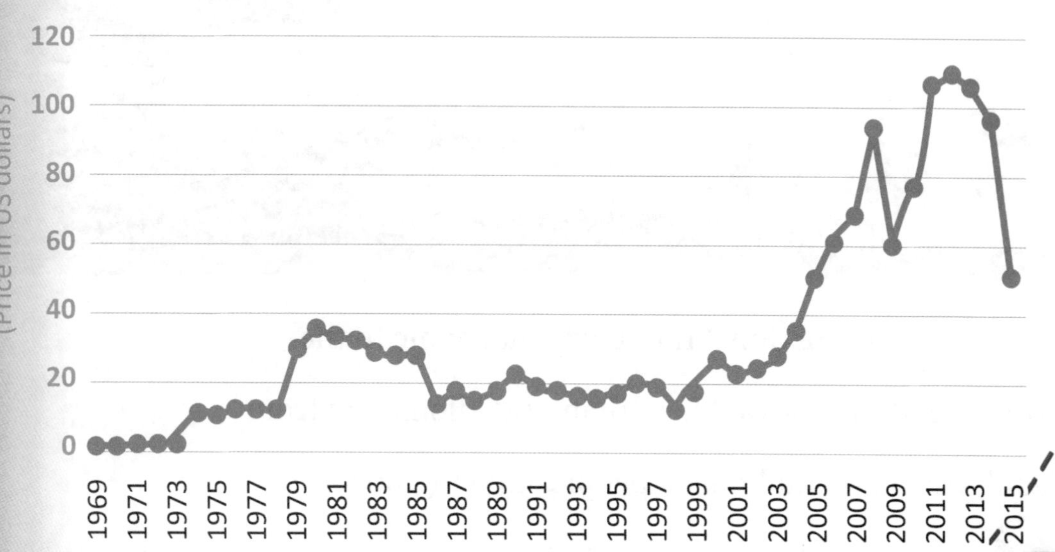

» skyrocket

Questions

_____ 1. What is this reading about?

a. Supply and demand. **b.** An important material.
c. A government. **d.** Household items.

_____ 2. Which of the following is not something that influences the price of oil?

a. The price of shampoo. **b.** Supply.
c. Public opinion. **d.** War.

_____ 3. What does it mean that governments are always "**on edge**"?

a. They are careful. **b.** They are worried.
c. They are taking risks. **d.** They are too big.

_____ 4. During which year did a war most likely break out in an oil-producing country?

a. 1983 **b.** 1991 **c.** 1979 **d.** 1971

_____ 5. Which year likely had the most oil available on the market?

a. 1973 **b.** 2011 **c.** 1981 **d.** 2014

22 Korea's Boryeong Mud Festival

22

Have any plans for July? If not, why not come to the Boryeong Mud Festival? Less than 200 kilometers from Seoul, you'll find millions of people enjoying Boryeong's mud on Daechon Beach from the 17th to the 26th.

Who attends?

Each year, the population of the small town of Boryeong rises from about 100,000 to millions of people. Koreans, foreign workers, and international visitors make up this population, making this a well-known world festival. Regardless of where you are from, **everyone is welcome to let loose** and enjoy some fun in the mud!

︽ mud pool

» fireworks

Questions

_____ 1. What is this reading about?

- **a.** A beach party for Westerners.
- **b.** Cosmetics made from mud.
- **c.** A festival held in Korea every year.
- **d.** The history of the mud beach in Boryeong.

_____ 2. Which of the following statements is true?

- **a.** There are fireworks every night of the festival.
- **b.** Most people who go to the festival are from Seoul.
- **c.** The festival is not a good place to bring children.
- **d.** Boryeong mud is good for your skin and body.

Why Mud?

The mud from Boryeong is healthy for your skin and body, and this has been proven by research. In fact, the first festival was held in 1998 so people could learn more about Boryeong mud cosmetics. The event was so popular, **it** was turned into an annual celebration.

Attractions

- *Mud Slides*
- *Colored Mud Face Painting*
- *Mud Pools*
- *Mud Sports*
- *Live Music*
- *Fireworks (last night only)*
- *Mud Cosmetics*

Daechon Beach (cc by catiemagee)

Don't wait!

Start planning your trip to beautiful Boryeong now!

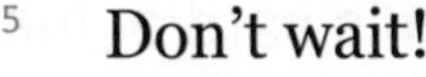

_____ **3.** What does "**everyone is welcome to let loose**" mean in the reading?

a. People should be careful not to lose things.

b. People who attend should act crazy.

c. People are invited to feel free.

d. People who go are welcome to dance.

_____ **4.** Where might you see this article in real life?

a. In a magazine. **b.** On television. **c.** In a comic book. **d.** In a novel.

_____ **5.** What does "**it**" mean?

a. The festival. **b.** Research. **c.** Mud cosmetics. **d.** Boryeong.

23 (23)

Bike Rentals

Thank you for your interest in the iBike system! Use your metro card to rent a bike and then **drop** it off at any other station around the city. **First things first**. Place your card on the reader below. If there's a problem, please see the instructions below.

Error Code	Message	How to Fix
0	**Cannot read your card.**	Try again. If there is still a problem, try another card.
1	**Card has not been registered.**	Please register your card at the nearest iBike computer screen.
2	**Card is already in use.**	Someone else is using this card at the moment. If you have just returned an iBike, please wait two minutes and try again.
3	**Card's balance is not sufficient.**	There is not enough money on your card. Please add money and try again.
4	**Card doesn't match.**	The card used to rent the iBike and the one used to return it don't match. Use the other card.
5	**Machine is unavailable.**	The iBike system is down at the moment. Please wait and try again in a few minutes. Sorry for the inconvenience.

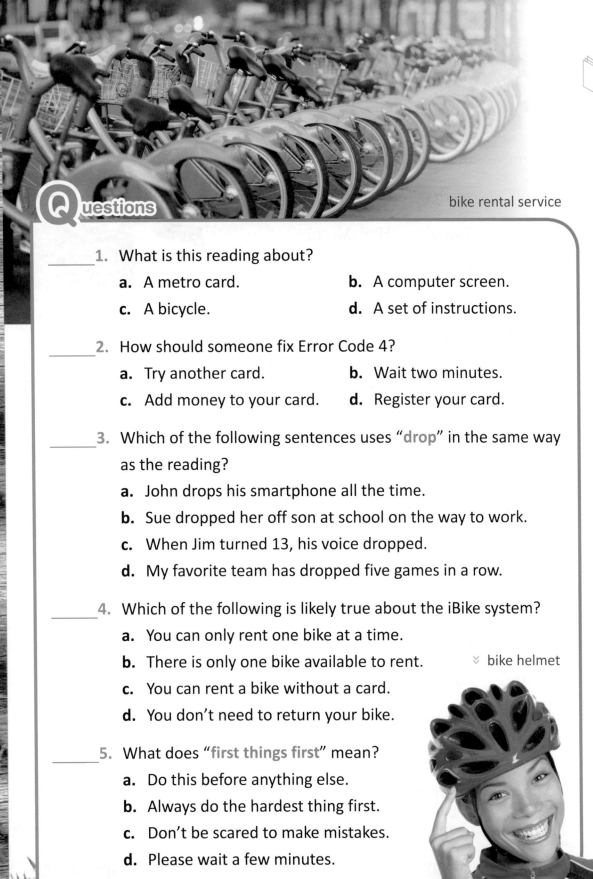

bike rental service

Questions

_____ 1. What is this reading about?

a. A metro card. b. A computer screen.
c. A bicycle. d. A set of instructions.

_____ 2. How should someone fix Error Code 4?

a. Try another card. b. Wait two minutes.
c. Add money to your card. d. Register your card.

_____ 3. Which of the following sentences uses "**drop**" in the same way as the reading?

a. John drops his smartphone all the time.
b. Sue dropped her off son at school on the way to work.
c. When Jim turned 13, his voice dropped.
d. My favorite team has dropped five games in a row.

_____ 4. Which of the following is likely true about the iBike system?

a. You can only rent one bike at a time.
b. There is only one bike available to rent.
c. You can rent a bike without a card.
d. You don't need to return your bike.

bike helmet

_____ 5. What does "**first things first**" mean?

a. Do this before anything else.
b. Always do the hardest thing first.
c. Don't be scared to make mistakes.
d. Please wait a few minutes.

24 Cleaning Your Teeth: A History

Mom: Jeannie, don't forget to brush your teeth before you go to bed, okay?

Jeannie: I won't . . . Hey, Mom?

Mom: What is it?

Jeannie: What did people do before toothbrushes and toothpaste? How did they keep their teeth clean?

^ brush teeth

Mom: Good question. **Why don't we look it up** online? Let's see here . . .

Jeannie : Okay, this **site** says that before the toothbrush was invented, people used to use rough cloths or sticks. And even today, some people in the Middle East and Africa still use small sticks to clean their teeth. They break them in half and rub the broken ends on their teeth!

Mom : What did people use instead of toothpaste?

Jeannie: Lots of different things: spices, salt, chalk, ash . . . But it also says that in the past, people's diets were much lower in sugar, so they didn't need to take as much care of their teeth.

Mom: Interesting. There are still some traditional societies where the people hardly ever need to brush their teeth because they don't eat any Western food! So, does that answer your question?

Jeannie: Yep! Thanks, Mom. Goodnight.

Questions

_____ 1. Which of the following do Jeannie and her mother talk about?
  a. How people took out bad teeth in the past.
  b. The person who invented the toothbrush.
  c. How often you should brush your teeth.
  d. Old-time ways of cleaning your teeth.

_____ 2. Which of the following is stated in the reading?
  a. People in the past ate more sugar than we do now.
  b. Chalk was once used as a kind of toothpaste.
  c. Some people in America still clean their teeth with sticks.
  d. People used to wash their mouths out with soap.

_____ 3. What does "**site**" mean here?
  a. A place to build a house. **b.** A famous work of art.
  c. A Web page. **d.** The ability to see.

_____ 4. What does the reading suggest about Western food?
  a. It's bad for your teeth. **b.** It's naturally low in sugar.
  c. It can't be avoided. **d.** It can help prevent bad teeth.

_____ 5. What does Jeannie's mother mean when she says, "**Why don't we look it up . . .?** "
  a. Let's try our best. **b.** Let's see what happens.
  c. Let's find the answer. **d.** Let's not bother.

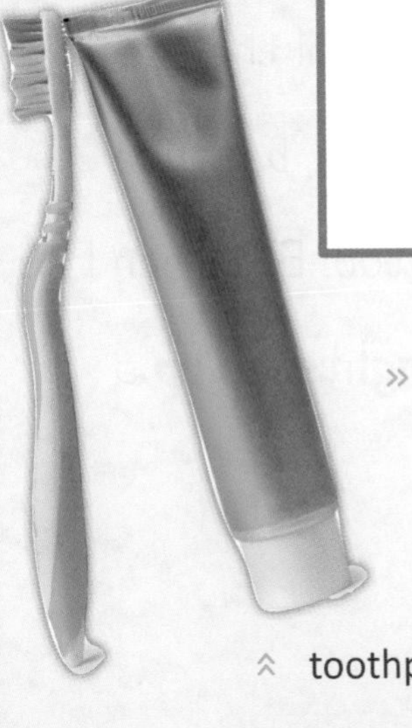

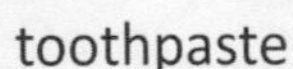

25 Mothers in the Animal Kingdom

25

Dear Diary,

Today was a pretty interesting day at school. It's Mother's Day today, so lots of our lessons had a Mother's Day theme. We learned about the history of Mother's Day in history class, Mother's Day in different cultures in our sociology class, and we read a Mother's Day poem in English. But my favorite lesson today was biology.

We learned about mothers in the animal kingdom. Some animals really **have it tough**! For example, some deep-sea octopuses guard their eggs for over four years, and they hardly eat at all while they're doing so. Some sharks—I think it was the frilled shark—carry their babies for three and a half years before they're born! I told Mom and she said, "Rather them than me!" I also told Mom about scorpions. After they give birth to their babies, scorpions carry them around on their backs until they're grown up. Mom said she sometimes feels like a scorpion, because she's always driving my sisters and me everywhere, too! But then I gave her a box of chocolates and a card, and she **brightened up** a bit after that.

Right; now off to bed.

Goodnight, Diary!

Frilled sharks carry their babies for three and a half years before they're born.

biology

Questions

_______ 1. What is the reading mainly about?

a. Interesting things the writer learned today.
b. The writer's mother.
c. How the writer celebrates Mother's Day.
d. The writer's favorite class at school.

_______ 2. What is said in the reading?

a. The writer wrote his mother a poem.
b. Scorpions carry their babies on their backs.
c. Octopuses eat their own eggs.
d. The writer's mother is a taxi driver.

_______ 3. What does it mean to "**have it tough**"?

a. Life is difficult for you.
b. You can't be beaten in a fight.
c. You have a hard head.
d. Fighting is your favorite thing.

_______ 4. What can we guess about the writer's mother?

a. She doesn't like chocolates.
b. She thinks sharks have an easy life.
c. She's a busy mother.
d. She's very lazy.

_______ 5. How do you feel if you "**brighten up**"?

a. Sadder. b. Smarter. c. Angrier. d. Happier.

octopus

scorpion with babies

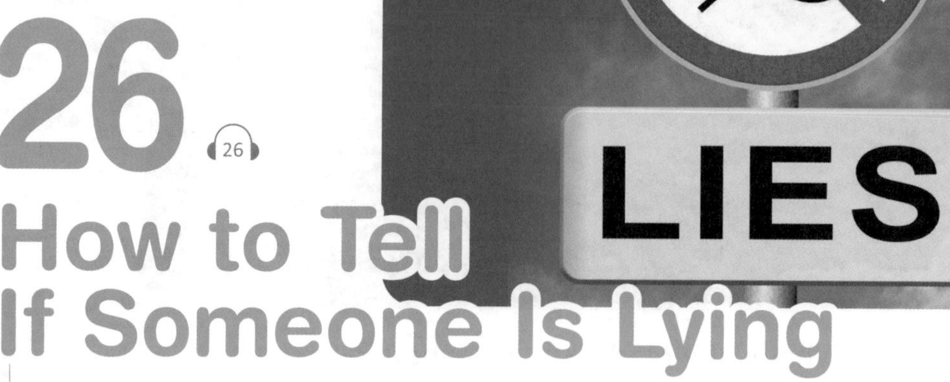

26 How to Tell If Someone Is Lying

If you say that you never lie, you are probably lying. The truth is that most people lie at least once during a 10-minute conversation. Maybe you have lied to protect someone, or to save someone from embarrassment. Maybe you have lied for selfish reasons—to make yourself **appear in a better light**, for example. Whether you have lied for good or for bad, we all lie.

⌃ tilt head

So how can we get to the truth? Researchers have come up with some **tell-tale** signs that may help you to spot lies (or maybe become better at telling them!).

- Eye Contact—making too little or too much eye contact while speaking
- Too Much Information—providing too many details and information not asked for
- Repetition—saying the same words or phrases over and over (e.g., "It wasn't me, it wasn't me")

» Touching the mouth is a common gesture people make when they're lying.

- Head Position—changing head position by tilting head to the side or pulling it back
- Body Movement—moving too much while standing or sitting, or not moving at all
- Touching the Mouth—touching or covering the mouth when asked a question

» eye contact

Questions

______ 1. What is the main idea of this reading?

a. Everyone lies from time to time.
b. People lie for many different reasons.
c. Researchers are trying to find out why people lie.
d. There are ways to tell if people are lying.

______ 2. Which of the following statements is true?

a. People usually lie for selfish reasons.
b. People always touch their mouths when they lie.
c. All lies are told for bad reasons.
d. Just about everyone lies.

______ 3. What does "**appear in a better light**" mean in the reading?

a. Look good. **b.** Ignore what people say about you.
c. Get ready for a talent show. **d.** Appear to be a greedy person.

______ 4. Who would find the skill of spotting lies on the job most useful?

a. A musician. **b.** A waitress. **c.** A sailor. **d.** A police officer.

______ 5. What does "**tell-tale**" mean?

a. Clear. **b.** Secret. **c.** Dishonest. **d.** Interesting.

gamers

Grand Theft Auto V

27 Planet Gamer

People who play video games, or "gamers," are becoming more and more common around the world. In fact, worldwide video game sales were worth over $93 billion in 2013. One game called *Grand Theft Auto V* sold 33 million copies worldwide, for a total of $2 billion in sales. That's more than a popular movie like *The Avengers*, which **made** "just" $1.5 billion at the box office.

The Avengers

Two segments of the global gaming industry are experiencing high growth. The first is mobile games, which are games that people play on their smartphones. You may have noticed everyone on the subway tapping away at his or her phone. MMORPGs are the other growing segment. MMORPGs offer an online world in which hundreds, even thousands, of real people can explore and go on adventures.

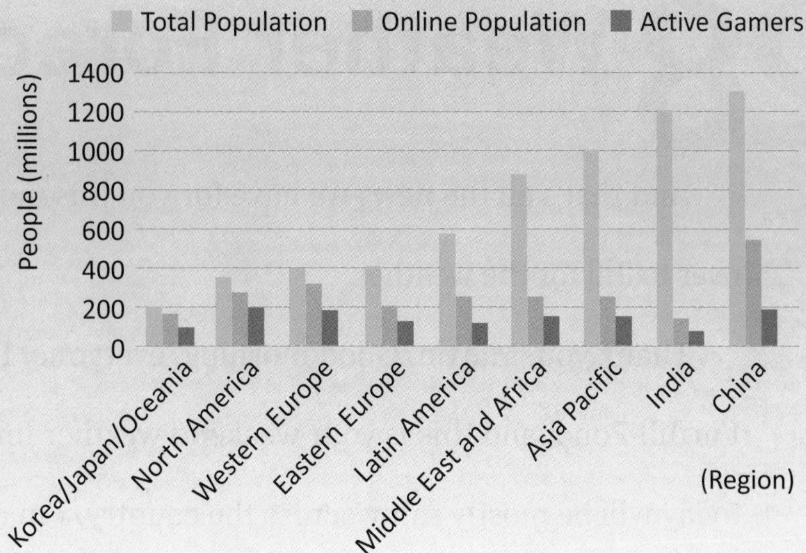

Questions

_____ 1. What does the chart show?

a. Where in the world gamers live.

b. What gamers around the world like to play.

c. The age of gamers around the world.

d. How much gamers around the world spend.

_____ 2. Which of the following regions has the largest population?

a. Latin America. b. North America.

c. Western Europe. d. Middle East and Africa.

_____ 3. Which of the following sentences uses "**made**" in the same way as the reading?

a. They made their flight at the last second.

b. He made a lot of money at his last job.

c. Mom made a pretty bag for me.

d. Seeing garbage on the floor made her angry.

_____ 4. Where are video games most popular?

a. China. b. India.

c. Middle East and Africa. d. North America.

_____ 5. Which region has the largest number of web users?

a. Korea/Japan/Oceania. b. North America.

c. China. d. India.

28 Weather Forecast

28

And that's all the news we have for you this morning, so now it's over to Jill for the weather.

Thank you, Martin. Good morning, everyone. It's Friday, May 5th, I'm Jill Pond, and this is your weekend weather forecast. The weather today will be mostly rainy across the country, I'm afraid. Heavy rain for the morning and most of the afternoon in the north and northeast, easing up a little as we go into this evening. The northwest can expect much of the same in the morning, but the weather should **brighten up** this afternoon and maybe we'll even see some strong sunshine later in the day. No such luck for those living in the south, however, as heavy

Questions

_____ **1.** What is Jill's talk about?

a. The best time to go for a picnic.
b. The weather over the coming days.
c. The country's southern region.
d. How the weather is changing with the season.

_____ **2.** What does Jill suggest about the weather on Friday morning in the northwest?

a. It will rain heavily.
b. There will be sun and a few clouds.
c. It will be very hot and sunny.
d. There will be heavy storms.

_____ **3.** What does Jill mean when she says the weather will "**brighten up**"?

a. It will be very hot.
b. It will begin to snow.
c. It will stop raining.
d. There will be no clouds.

storms will be passing over the entire southern region all day and well into the evening.

Moving into tomorrow and Sunday, though, we can expect an **about-face** from the weather. Sun and few clouds for all of Saturday and Sunday in all areas. It'll be nice and warm throughout the day, with temperatures of about 70 degrees Fahrenheit—perfect weather for a picnic! That's all from me. Have a great weekend.

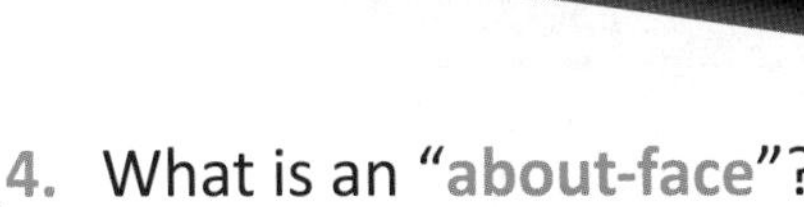

» weather forecast

_____ 4. What is an "**about-face**"?

a. A similar pattern.
b. A complete stop.
c. A long wait.
d. A complete change.

_____ 5. On Saturday, my girlfriend and I went out for the day. I took a picture of her. Which one is it?

a. 

b. 

c. 

d. 

29

29 Daily Horoscope

Aries
March 21 – April 19

You'll meet someone important today. Make sure you make a good first impression.

Taurus
April 20 – May 20

Stay away from people with beards. Someone with facial hair is **out to get you.**

Gemini
May 21 – June 20

Someone close to you is celebrating something big. Don't forget to congratulate him or her. Forgetting to do so will mean losing a close friend.

Libra
September 23 – October 22

Today you'll meet the man or woman of your dreams. **Don't let this person pass you by.**

Scorpio
October 23 – November 21

Call your parents. You'll be glad you did.

Sagittarius
November 22 – December 21

You have a big task to do today, but it's bound to go wrong. Put it off until tomorrow.

Questions

_____ **1.** What can you learn about from the reading?

a. Your past. **b.** Your future.
c. Your previous lives. **d.** Your dreams.

_____ **2.** My star sign is Capricorn. According to the reading, what should I do today?

a. Call my mom. **b.** Avoid anything dangerous.
c. Take up skydiving. **d.** Give my wife some flowers.

_____ **3.** I read my horoscope, and as a result I'm not leaving the house today. Which star sign am I?

a. Pisces. **b.** Libra. **c.** Gemini. **d.** Leo.

Cancer
June 21 – July 22

It's a good day for trying something new. Do something you've never done before and good things are sure to follow.

Leo
July 23 – August 22

The stars have only bad things in store for you today. It's best that you stay home.

Virgo
August 23 – September 22

You're in danger of having an accident. Be extra careful today.

Capricorn
December 22 – January 19

If you give a small gift to a loved one today, it will make your relationship a lot stronger.

Aquarius
January 20 – February 18

Someone will try to bully you today. Stand up for yourself. It will lead to a big change in your life.

Pisces
February 19 – March 20

Today you'll have the chance to get back at someone. Don't take it. It will lead to ruin.

_____ **4.** What does it mean if someone is "**out to get you**"?

- **a.** He or she wants to sell you something.
- **b.** He or she wants to make you happy.
- **c.** He or she wants to hurt you.
- **d.** He or she wants to give you advice.

_____ **5.** What does the phrase "**Don't let this person pass you by**" mean?

- **a.** Make sure you notice this person.
- **b.** Don't let this person beat you.
- **c.** Don't make friends with this person.
- **d.** Stay away from this person at all costs.

30 SkinGlow Sheet Mask

SkinGlow

Facial Sheet Mask

Green Tea

This new mask from SkinGlow contains natural green tea extract, which helps keep your skin looking and feeling fresh, reduces the appearance of fine lines, and stops your skin from drying out.

Directions:

» peel away

1 Clean your face with soap and warm water.
2 Open the pack and take out the mask.
3 Peel away the film from the back of the mask.
4 Apply the mask to your face, starting at the top and moving down.
5 Pat the mask lightly with your hands to get rid of any air pockets.
6 Leave the mask on for 15–20 minutes.
7 Remove the mask and rub any liquid that's left over into the skin.

For best results, use once or twice a week.

Caution:

» fine lines

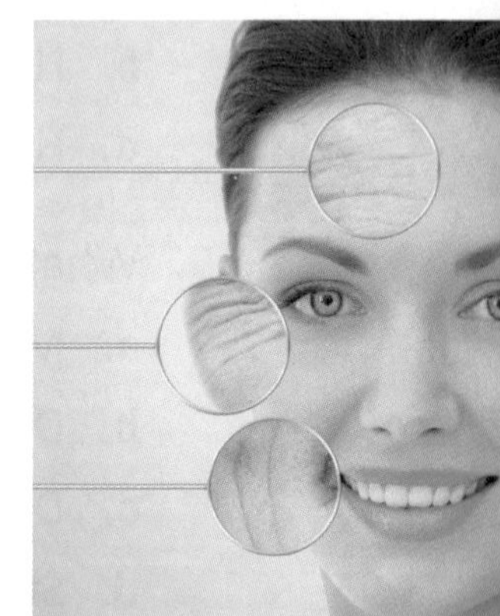

1 Stop using the mask right away if it causes your skin to become red or irritated.
2 Do not use on broken or irritated skin.
3 Avoid direct contact with eyes. If irritation occurs, rinse eyes right away with water.

« facial sheet mask » irritated

Questions

_____ 1. What does the reading tell you about the SkinGLow facial sheet mask?

a. How to use it. b. What people think of it.
c. How it is made. d. Why it's better than similar masks.

_____ 2. I've put the mask on, but some parts aren't sticking to my skin. What should I do?

a. Wash my face with soap and water.
b. Pat the mask lightly with my hands.
c. Take the mask off right away.
d. Ignore it and leave it as it is.

_____ 3. What does the word "**caution**" mean?

a. Go ahead. b. Try harder. c. Be careful. d. Save time.

_____ 4. This mask was probably designed for someone with what type of skin?

a. Dark skin. b. Pale skin. c. Burned skin. d. Dry skin.

_____ 5. What is Dana doing wrong?

Dear SkinGlow,
I've been using your Green Tea facial sheet mask for a while now, but my skin doesn't feel any different. I use the mask once a month, and I follow all the directions on the pack. But my skin still looks and feels dull, and none of my lines has disappeared. Am I doing something wrong?
Yours sincerely,
Dana Beach

a. She's applying the mask incorrectly.
b. She has the wrong skin type.
c. She's not using the mask often enough.
d. She's using the mask too often.

31 Can Cockroaches Survive Without Their Heads?

31

If you've ever had a cockroach in your house, you'll **know first-hand** how hard they are to kill. Sometimes even stamping on a cockroach isn't enough to kill it. It's also been said that they can survive a nuclear bomb. And now scientists have discovered that these amazing insects can stay alive even after getting their heads cut off!

˄ cockroaches

˅ insects

The reason for this is that, unlike humans, cockroaches don't breathe through their mouths. Instead, a cockroach breathes through tiny holes all over its body. Also unlike a human, a cockroach has a tiny "mini-brain" in each part of its body. This means that even without a head, it can still feel and move around. And, to top it all off, cockroaches don't need nearly as much food as humans do. A cockroach can live for weeks on just one meal.

Although their bodies will die **sooner or later**, headless cockroaches have been known to stay alive for several weeks! Even stranger, their heads can stay alive, too! A cockroach's head will keep waving its antennae for hours after being separated from its body. This probably makes the cockroach the toughest living thing on the planet!

Questions

_____ **1.** Which of the following facts is the writer's main focus?

a. Cockroaches are difficult to kill.

b. Cockroaches can stay alive even without their heads.

c. Cockroach brains aren't like human brains.

d. Cockroaches can live for a long time without food.

_____ **2.** Which of the following is said about cockroaches?

a. They have three stomachs.

b. They eat through little holes all over their bodies.

c. They don't breathe through their mouths.

d. They don't have a brain.

_____ **3.** What does it mean to "**know something first-hand**"?

a. You know it by touch.

b. Someone described it to you in writing.

c. You were the first person to know it.

d. You've experienced it personally.

_____ **4.** What does the writer mean by "**sooner or later**"?

a. At some point. **b.** Right away. **c.** Never. **d.** Earlier than expected.

_____ **5.** Which of these is probably the author's opinion?

a. Killing cockroaches is cruel.

b. Cockroaches are very surprising animals.

c. People should not eat cockroaches.

d. Cockroaches aren't very interesting.

32 Lost and Found Notice

DID YOU LOSE SOMETHING?

First of all, thank you to everyone who attended the school Christmas party last night! We hope you all had a great time. Some of you, though, were having such a great time that you forgot some of your stuff! During clean-up, the cleaning team found the following items in and around the school gym:

A brown leather jacket

A black baseball cap with an orange star on the front

A set of keys on a pink teddy-bear keychain

A subway travel card in a "Hello Kitty" card holder

One small silver earring, shaped like a heart

A thin black necktie

If one or more of these items belongs to you, please see Mrs. Jenkins, the school secretary, in the school office in Building D.

IMPORTANT

To reclaim your **possessions**, please bring a signed note from one of your parents to confirm that the item belongs to you.

If after 10 days no one has claimed a particular item, it will be **donated to a charity** for homeless children.

Thank you for your attention,

The Christmas Party Committee

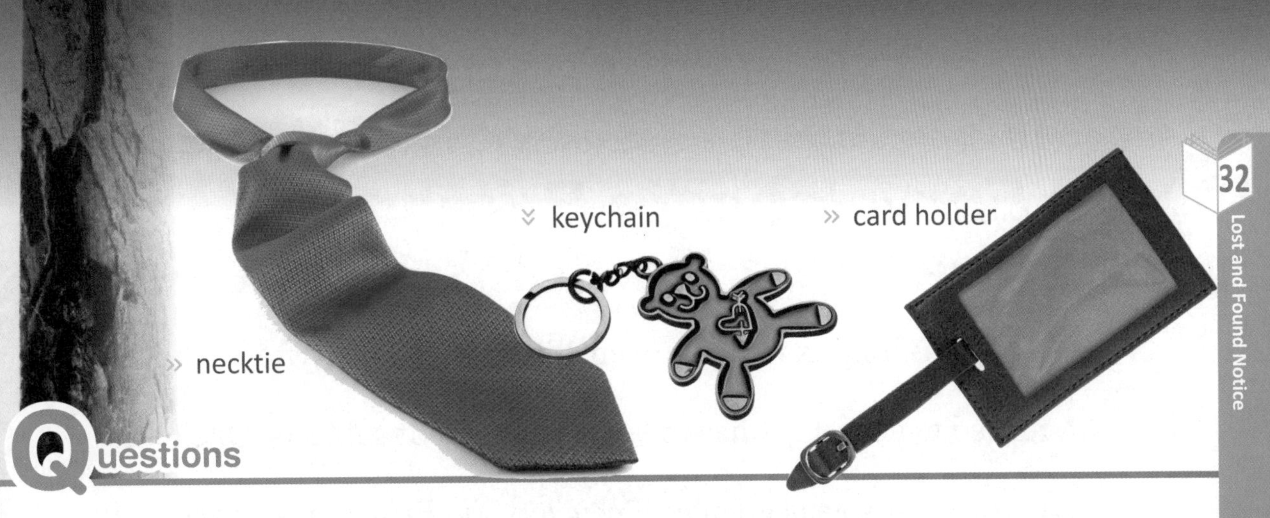

Questions

_____ 1. The list of items in the notice is a list of what?

a. Thank-you gifts for people who helped clean up after the party.

b. Prizes that students can win if they attended the Christmas party.

c. Things that were left behind at the school's Christmas party.

d. Things that are needed to decorate the gym for the Christmas party.

_____ 2. Which of these is not one of the items on the list?

a. 

b. 

c. 

d. 

_____ 3. What does "**possession**" mean?

a. Something that you want to give away.
b. Something you'd like to buy.
c. Something that belongs to you.
d. Something you borrowed.

_____ 4. Why do students need to show a note from their parents before they can get their things back?

a. To stop students from claiming things that aren't theirs.

b. To make students be more careful next time.

c. To prove students are who they say they are.

d. To make students not want to get their items back.

_____ 5. What does it mean if something is "**donated to a charity**"?

a. It's given away for a good cause.
b. It's put into a storeroom.
c. It's thrown into the garbage.
d. It's used to decorate a room.

» *Britannica*'s logo

33 *Encyclopedia Britannica*: The Most Useful Books Around

For as long as we have been able to read and write, we have turned to encyclopedias to learn more about subjects. One of the most famous ones is called *Encyclopedia Britannica*. It was first published in 1768 in the United Kingdom. At first *Britannica* was a collection of essays on different topics, many of them having to do with science. However, after the first edition sold out **in no time**, the publishers decided to make the second edition bigger. Now it included key events in history and the life stories of famous people.

« 15th edition of the *Britannica*
(cc by SEWilco)

Encyclopedias used to be an important way of spreading new information about history and science. Remember that people couldn't just look things up on the computer back then! Speaking of which, *Encyclopedia Britannica* has also made the jump online. That means you can tap into its deep pool of knowledge in the library or on the go.

Questions

_____ **1.** What is the main idea of this reading?

a. Encyclopedias are very old.
b. Encyclopedias have essays on science.
c. *Britannica* is a famous encyclopedia.
d. *Britannica* is published in the United Kingdom.

_____ **2.** Which of the following is true about *Encyclopedia Britannica*?

a. It only had one edition.
b. It only has essays on science.
c. It is now online.
d. It was first printed in 1748.

_____ **3.** What does it mean that the first edition of *Britannica* sold out "**in no time**"?

a. It did not sell out.
b. It was not sold in stores.
c. It did not sell any copies.
d. It sold out quickly.

_____ **4.** In which volume would you find an essay on trains?

a. Volume 5. **b.** Volume 6. **c.** Volume 7. **d.** Volume 8.

_____ **5.** If you wanted to know more about hyenas, which volume would you check?

a. Volume 3. **b.** Volume 4. **c.** Volume 5. **d.** Volume 6.

34 Ice Queen

“One of the most exciting and charming stories ever told.”

–Jim Brown, *Film Magazine*

“**Fun for adults and children alike.**”

–Jerry Bright, *Movie Talk*

Ice Queen

In Lapuland, summer never comes. It has been winter for as long as anyone can remember. A brave young farm girl called Annabelle sets off on a journey to find the cause of Lapuland’s endless winter. With the help of a handsome hunter, Biglaf, and his trusty dog, Mitten, Annabelle travels to the Frosty Mountains, the home of the Ice Queen. But the road is a dangerous one. Can Anabelle and her friends make it across the frozen mountains safely? And what will they do when faced with the queen’s army of fierce white bears?

This wonderful story takes you on a magical journey to save a kingdom. It’s fun for the whole family!

Bring home *Ice Queen* on Blu-ray and you’ll get a lot of never-before-seen extras. On this Blu-ray disc you get interviews with the actors, deleted scenes, and a whole different ending to the movie!

Questions

_____1. What is the purpose of the reading?

a. To let you know Ice Queen is a family movie.

b. To tell you what Jerry Bright thought about the movie.

c. To tell you about the movie's ending.

d. To get you interested in the movie.

_____2. Which of the following is said about Lapuland?

a. It's ruled by a handsome king.

b. It's always winter there.

c. Only bears live there.

d. It's by the seaside.

_____3. What does the phrase "**Fun for adults and children alike**" mean?

a. Everyone will enjoy this movie, no matter how old he or she is.

b. Only adults will enjoy this movie; children won't like it.

c. This movie is fun for children, but not for adults.

d. Neither adults nor children will like this movie.

_____4. Who is the main character in the movie?

a. The Ice Queen. b. Biglaf.

c. Annabelle. d. Mitten.

_____5. What can we guess about the Ice Queen?

a. She's not human.

b. She's the hero of the story.

c. She's the evil character in the movie.

d. She's Annabelle's mother.

» What's inside of blood, a Khan academy video (cc by Butterfinger8181)

» Khan Academy's logo

35 KHANACADEMY

The Khan Academy

35

How many students does the average teacher teach in a lifetime? Thousands, certainly. But tens of thousands? Millions? Probably not. Salman Khan is a teacher, too—with over 25 million students.

But how can **one man** teach so many people? With the help of the Internet, of course. Salman Khan is the **founder** of the Khan Academy, an online organization dedicated to providing anyone, anywhere, with a free, world-class education.

The project began when Khan, who has degrees from both MIT and Harvard, began teaching his cousin mathematics over the Internet. Many of Khan's other relatives wanted his help, too, so he decided to begin making educational videos and posting them online.

The academy's website features links to over 2,400 courses, covering subjects from math to the history of art. The lessons take the form of YouTube videos followed by several practice exercises.

« Salman Khan (born 1976) (cc by Steve Jurvetson)

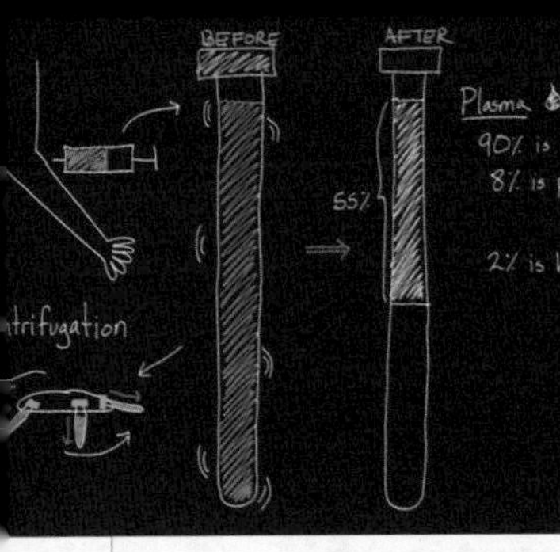

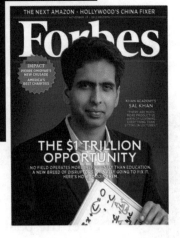

» *Forbes* magazine featured Khan on its cover.

One of the most important things about these videos is that they're available in languages other than English. At present, Khan's lessons are available in 65 languages. This means that anyone can use the service, no matter where he or she is from, what language he or she speaks, or how much money he or she has.

Questions

_____ **1.** What is the reading's main message?

- **a.** The Khan Academy has courses on many subjects.
- **b.** The Khan Academy is like a regular school.
- **c.** The Khan Academy provides free education to the world.
- **d.** The Khan academy has over 25 million students.

_____ **2.** What is said about Salman Khan?

- **a.** He's American.
- **b.** He has a good education.
- **c.** He's a young man.
- **d.** He speaks many languages.

_____ **3.** If I am the "**founder**" of an organization, what did I do?

- **a.** Buy it.
- **b.** Start it.
- **c.** Sell it.
- **d.** Learn from it.

_____ **4.** Who does the Khan Academy help most?

- **a.** People in poor countries.
- **b.** People who have been to college.
- **c.** People who work in business.
- **d.** People who don't like studying.

_____ **5.** Who is "**one man**"?

- **a.** Khan's cousin.
- **b.** The average teacher.
- **c.** One of Khan's students.
- **d.** Salman Khan.

36 Time to Disconnect 36

Technology: Time to Disconnect?

By Professor R. J. Howard

Over the past few years, technology has developed at an unbelievable speed. We are now at a point where we have a whole world of entertainment and communication **at our fingertips** at all times. But are these mini-computers that we always carry around in our pockets good for us? Do they make us more connected with each other? Or do they disconnect us from reality? The idea to write this book came from a study performed by a friend of mine, Professor T. M. Stark, in late 2013. Professor Stark wanted to examine his students' ability to focus on a task. He found that students who checked Facebook often got lower grades and found it more difficult to focus on their work. Professor Stark's study got me thinking: is technology changing us for the better, or for the worse? As a great lover of modern technology, I found this book difficult and sometimes painful to write. But here it is—technology, **warts and all**. I hope that by reading this book you too will understand the damage that an addiction to technology can cause.

March 2015

Facebook

Technology has changed our lives.

Questions

_____ 1. What is the writer trying to express to the reader?

a. His love for technology.
b. His respect for his friend Professor Stark.
c. His reasons for writing a book.
d. The speed at which technology is developing.

_____ 2. What gave the writer the idea for his book?

a. A bad experience he had with technology as a child.
b. A study showing the negative effects of technology on students.
c. A conversation he had with a co-worker.
d. A book about the wonderful things technology has done for us.

_____ 3. Which of these describes something that's "**at one's fingertips**"?

a. It's hard to understand.
b. It's difficult to use.
c. It's cheap to buy.
d. It's easy to get at.

_____ 4. If you asked Professor Howard what his opinion of technology was, what would he most likely say?

a. "It's great, but you can have too much of a good thing."
b. "It's the worst thing that has ever happened to us."
c. "It's great, harmless fun. The more you use it, the better!"
d. "I don't think it affects us very much at all."

_____ 5. What does it mean to show something "**warts and all**"?

a. You show only the good things.
b. You show everything, even the unpleasant things.
c. You provide only a very general picture.
d. You tell people exactly what they want to hear.

Mark Twain in his D. Litt. (Doctor of Letters) academic dress, awarded by Oxford University

Mark Twain, age 15

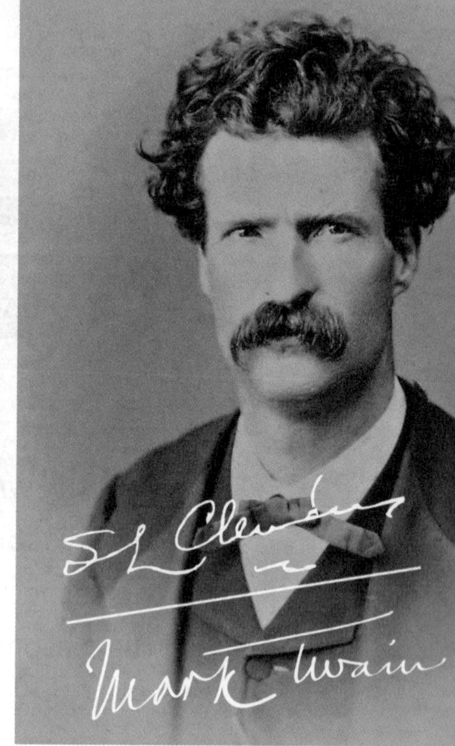

Mark Twain in 1867

37 Mark Twain

Mark Twain in 1895

Mark Twain is known as one of America's greatest writers. He was born in 1835 in Missouri and before becoming a writer worked as a journalist, a miner, and a riverboat pilot on the Mississippi.

He is perhaps most famous for writing *The Adventures of Huckleberry Finn*. The novel is set in the American South during the time when Americans still kept slaves. The story follows a young boy, Huck, and a runaway slave, Jim, on their adventures down the Mississippi River. One of Twain's greatest talents was his ability to write in dialects. *Huckleberry Finn* is written in a local dialect of the American South. The characters use lots of **colorful** language and slang terms, which makes them really come to life.

Twain also strongly disagreed with many ideas common in American society, particularly those about race. And he dealt with these issues in his novels. Though he died in 1910, his books are very popular to this day. You might even come across one of his stories in your English class. If you do, you're certainly in for a treat! Twain's ability to tell a story really is **second to none**!

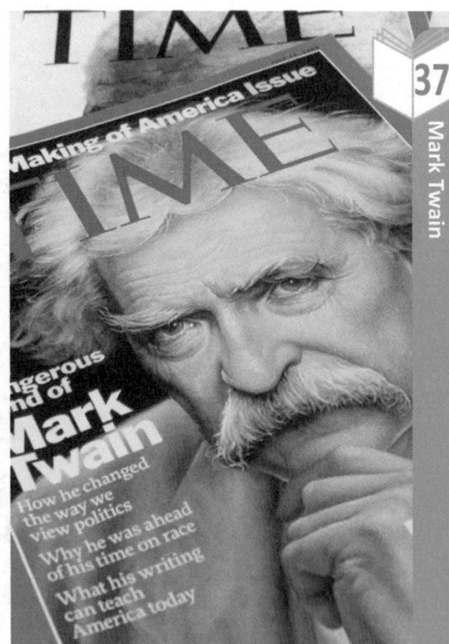

» *Time* magazine with Mark Twain's portrait on the cover

Questions

_____ 1. What is the reading mostly about?

- **a.** America's greatest writers.
- **b.** The life and work of an American writer.
- **c.** American ideas about race in the 19th century.
- **d.** The Mississippi River in English novels.

_____ 2. Which of these is said about *The Adventures of Huckleberry Finn*?

- **a.** It's about a journalist.
- **b.** The characters' speech is unique.
- **c.** It's set in the future.
- **d.** It's based on Mark Twain's life.

_____ 3. What does "**colorful**" mean here?

- **a.** Many-colored.
- **b.** Clear and simple.
- **c.** Interesting and exciting.
- **d.** Made-up.

_____ 4. What can we guess about Twain's time working on a riverboat?

- **a.** It influenced his writing.
- **b.** It made him a rich man.
- **c.** It caused his death.
- **d.** It gave him a deep fear of water.

_____ 5. If someone is "**second to none**" at something, what does it mean?

- **a.** He's OK at it, but not the best.
- **b.** He completes the task very quickly.
- **c.** He won a prize for doing it.
- **d.** No one does it better.

» props (= properties)

38

38 Everwood Science Fair

Come one, come all to the fourth annual

Everwood High School

Science Fair

Date/Time: May 29th, 9 a.m. to 4 p.m.

Place: Everwood High School Gym

It's that time of year again! Dust off your test tubes and wash your lab coats because the best and brightest of Everwood are **facing off**. This year's topic will be "the planet's next big energy source." First place will win a brand new microscope and a month off from school (not!). The **runner-up** will take home a NTD1,000 gift card for the Everwood Mall.

Rules:

1) Each entry must be on a white poster with large block letters for the project title.
2) Students can paste writing and pictures to their posters.
3) Each entry must have a written introduction explaining what the project is and why it's important.
4) Each entry must be based on a science experiment that the student did on his or her own.
5) Students can display props other than their posters so long as they have to do with their science experiments.
6) Parents are not allowed to help in any way.

« science fair project

» school gym

Questions

_____ 1. What is this reading about?

a. An experiment. b. An event. c. A school. d. A microscope.

_____ 2. Which of the following is not one of the rules of the science fair?

a. Parents can help with their child's entry.
b. Each student must do a science experiment.
c. Each entry must be on a white poster.
d. Students can use certain kinds of props.

_____ 3. What does it mean that the best and brightest are "**facing off**"?

a. They can see each other.
b. They go to the same school.
c. They are working against each other.
d. They are all very smart.

_____ 4. Which of the following subjects would be a good entry for the science fair?

a. "The life of African monkeys."
b. "How sunlight can power our homes."
c. "New ways to clean water."
d. "Why do farts smell so bad?"

_____ 5. Who is a "**runner-up**"?

a. Someone who trains every day.
b. Someone who watches the science fair.
c. Someone who doesn't like science.
d. Someone who comes in second.

» science experiment

39

» look up

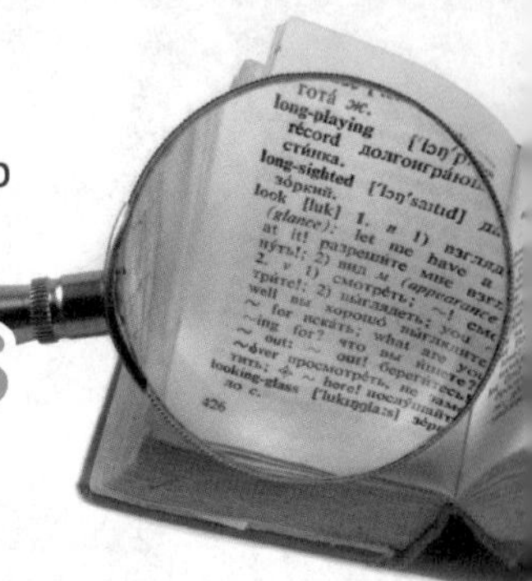

39 What on Earth Is Fish Paste ?

I was just looking through a cookbook, and I saw a dish I'd like to try to make—Thai-style fishcakes. They look delicious. One of the things I need, though, is something called "fish **paste**." I have no idea what it is. I know the word "**paste**" from the computer, where you "copy and paste" something. But here it's a noun, not a verb. I'd better **look it up** in the dictionary.

paste /pest/

noun

1. a soft, wet mixture, usually made of a powder and a liquid
2. crushed meat, fish, etc. that is spread on bread or used in cooking
3. a type of glue that is used for sticking things to paper
4. a material like glass used for making fake jewels, for example diamonds

fishcake

verb

1. paste something + adv./prep.—to stick something to something else using glue or paste
2. paste something—to make something by sticking pieces of paper together
3. paste (something) (computers)—to copy or move information from another place

fish paste

Questions

_____ 1. Why does the writer need to use the dictionary?

a. He doesn't know how to spell a word.
b. He doesn't know how to pronounce a word.
c. He wants to know where a word comes from.
d. He wants to find out what a word means.

_____ 2. Which meaning of the word "**paste**" does the writer already know?

a. To stick something to something else using glue or paste.
b. To copy or move information from another place.
c. Crushed meat, fish, etc. that is spread on bread or used in cooking.
d. A soft, wet mixture, usually made of a powder and a liquid.

_____ 3. What do you do if you "**look something up**"?

a. Look at a book or computer in order to find information.
b. Feel happy and excited about something that's going to happen.
c. Take care of someone or something.
d. Visit a place and look at the things in it.

_____ 4. Which of the entries describes the word "**paste**" as used in the writer's cookbook?

a. noun; 1 **b.** noun; 2 **c.** verb; 1 **d.** verb; 2

_____ 5. Which of the following uses "paste" as described in the entry noun; 4?

a. Is that a real precious stone, or is it made of paste?
b. Next, apply some paste to the back of the wallpaper.
c. My favorite sandwich filling is chicken paste and boiled egg.
d. Take the flour and milk and mix them into a paste.

40 Blue Gold

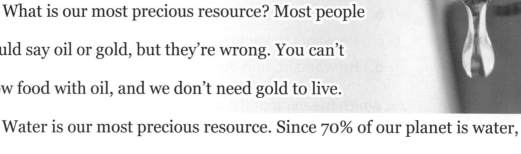

» leaking faucet

What is our most precious resource? Most people would say oil or gold, but they're wrong. You can't grow food with oil, and we don't need gold to live.

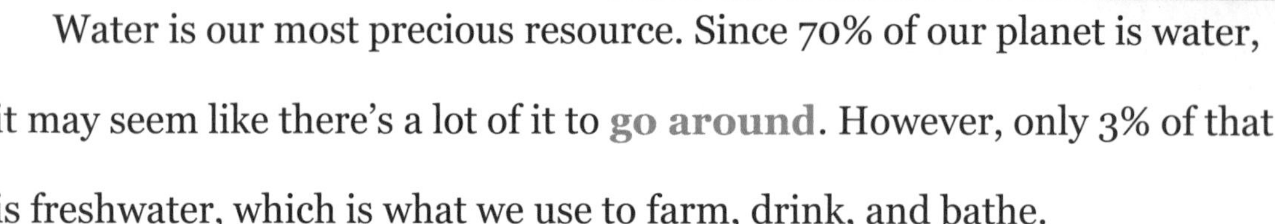

Water is our most precious resource. Since 70% of our planet is water, it may seem like there's a lot of it to **go around**. However, only 3% of that is freshwater, which is what we use to farm, drink, and bathe.

Around 1.2 billion people are already facing a shortage of freshwater. By the year 2025, this number is expected to increase to 1.8 billion. The problem is getting worse because of overpopulation, climate change, and people simply wasting water. For example, the US Environmental Protection Agency says that one trillion gallons are wasted every year by leaking faucets. That's enough water for 24 billion baths.

It's clear we all have **a role to play** in fixing the problem. The good news is it's not too hard. Try showering for one minute less and you'll save 150 gallons of water every month. Turning the water off when you brush your teeth will also save four gallons a minute.

» overpopulation

natural resources

Questions

_____ 1. What point is this reading trying to make?

a. Our planet is 70% water.
b. We can solve the water problem.
c. Oil is a precious resource.
d. We use freshwater to drink and bathe.

_____ 2. Which of the following wastes one trillion gallons of water in the United States every year?

a. Long showers.
b. Brushing teeth .
c. Baths.
d. Leaky faucets.

_____ 3. What does it mean that there's enough water to "**go around**"?

a. Water flows so it's easy to move around.
b. There is enough water for everyone.
c. There's too much water on the planet.
d. Water is something that everyone needs.

_____ 4. Which of the following is a tip that the US Environmental Protection Agency might give?

a. Eat apples instead of oranges.
b. Use rainwater in your toilet.
c. Use bottled water to wash your car.
d. Bathe your cats and dogs twice a day.

_____ 5. What does it mean that we all have "**a role to play**" in fixing the problem?

a. Everyone needs to use less water.
b. The water problem cannot be fixed.
c. There isn't enough water on the planet.
d. We should teach kids about water.

climate change

» "Checking in" allows people to share their daily comings and goings.

41 The Two Sides of "Checking In" on Facebook

social media

The rise of smartphones and Facebook has changed the way that we interact. It has also changed the way we view our privacy. We've invited a leading expert to discuss the **trend** of "checking in," or adding a location to Facebook posts.

Sarah: What's the big deal about checking in? People love it.

John: There's a lot that's good about it. It allows people to share their daily **comings and goings** with friends and family. It also allows local businesses to advertise with every check-in. But this all comes at a cost in terms of privacy.

Sarah: Sure, sure, we've heard this all before. Do you even realize that you can change your Facebook settings and control who sees your check-ins?

John: That's not the problem. The more worrying matter is how Facebook and these other online companies can collect your information. If that information includes where you eat, shop, and sleep, then it's very important. You may trust Facebook, but it can and will sell this information to a third party that you don't trust.

« interview

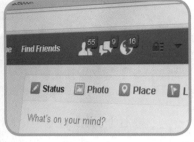

≈ notifications on Facebook

Questions

_____ 1. What is this article about?

- a. Facebook settings.
- b. Privacy.
- c. Smartphones.
- d. Shopping.

_____ 2. Why is John worried about people checking in on Facebook?

- a. It's too difficult to change the settings.
- b. It collects too much of your information.
- c. It costs too much time.
- d. It can be seen by your friends and family.

_____ 3. What are a person's "**comings and goings**"?

- a. His or her information.
- b. His or her privacy.
- c. His or her movements.
- d. His or her smartphone.

_____ 4. What does Sarah likely think about checking in?

- a. It's great.
- b. It's dangerous.
- c. It's not important.
- d. It's boring.

_____ 5. What does it mean that checking in is a "**trend**"?

- a. It's brand new.
- b. It's popular.
- c. It's complicated.
- d. It's not allowed.

42

Are Knock-Offs Really Worth It?

Fake handbags are widely and cheaply sold in Indonesia.

If I told you that you could buy a luxury item for much less than the original cost, would you be interested? What if I told you that although it isn't real, it looks and feels just like the real thing? Sounds like a great deal, doesn't it?

Each year, billions of dollars trade hands in the **underworld** of illegal knock-off goods. You may not realize it, but buying that knock-off Louis Vuitton bag or iPhone makes you part of this underworld.

Questions

_____ **1.** What is the purpose of this reading?

- **a.** To tell people how to save money when shopping.
- **b.** To let people know why people sell illegal goods.
- **c.** To tell people why they shouldn't buy knock-offs.
- **d.** To let people know about crime in their cities.

_____ **2.** Why does it matter to society if people who make and sell knock-offs don't pay taxes?

- **a.** If taxes aren't paid, workers don't earn fair pay.
- **b.** It doesn't matter because it's not hurting anyone.
- **c.** The original makers don't earn enough money.
- **d.** Places like hospitals and schools receive less money.

Fake brand-name watches in a black market in Myanmar.

illegal knock-off goods

You may be wondering, "So what if I have a knock-off? It's not hurting anyone, is it?" The answer may surprise you.

Many knock-offs are made in factories with poor working conditions where workers don't get fair pay. Some of these factories even use child workers. Also, the people who make money off the sale of knock-off goods don't pay taxes. This means your city receives less money for hospitals, schools, and other social facilities. You should also know that knock-off sales often support other kinds of crime, including drug activity and terrorism.

Doesn't sound like such a good deal anymore, does it?

_____ **3.** What does "**underworld**" mean in the reading?

- **a.** Poor working conditions in factories.
- **b.** The culture of crime and illegal activity.
- **c.** Places where people sell-knock offs.
- **d.** Factories where illegal goods are made.

_____ **4.** Where would you be most likely to find a knock-off item for sale?

- **a.** At an airport.
- **b.** At a department store.
- **c.** On a designer's website.
- **d.** At a night market.

_____ **5.** What is one reason people like to buy knock-offs?

- **a.** They are better than real luxury goods.
- **b.** Their sales improve social facilities.
- **c.** They help to create more jobs for children.
- **d.** They cost less than the real thing.

43 Job Application Email

April 24th, 2015

Dear Ms. Espinoza,

Hello! My name is Fred Stephens, and I am writing about your advertisement for a sales manager in today's *Daily News*. A copy of my resume is attached.

I graduated from Northwestern University with a degree in marketing in 2013. Since then I have been working as a sales assistant at Dynochip Computers in San Francisco. I like my job, and am told I'm doing very well in it. However, I really want a position which will let me take more control of meetings and travel more often. If I am given greater responsibility, I am sure I can achieve even greater results. Also, I am very interested in working in Europe, and used to dream of going to Spain after graduating. **We sound like a perfect match**, don't we?

Please reply to me as soon as possible at this email address. If I am hired, I can start work in one month. The job advertised by your office sounds like an exciting opportunity; I hope very much it can be mine.

Thank you for your time and have a wonderful day!

Sincerely yours,

Fred Stephens

« job application

» meeting

Questions

_____ 1. Why did Fred Stephens write this letter?

a. To talk about his dreams.
b. To apply for a university program.
c. To apply for a job.
d. To find a European pen pal.

_____ 2. Where did Fred find the advertisement he is answering?

a. In a newspaper.
b. At Northwestern University.
c. On television.
d. At Dynochip Computers.

_____ 3. What does Fred mean when he writes, "**We sound like a perfect match**"?

a. He wants to marry Ms. Espinoza.
b. He thinks that he and Ms. Espinoza look alike.
c. He and Ms. Espinoza both want to work in Europe.
d. He thinks he and Ms. Espinoza can work well together.

_____ 4. Where is Ms. Espinoza's office probably located?

a. In Taiwan.
b. At Northwestern University.
c. In Spain.
d. In San Francisco.

_____ 5. What did Fred send to Ms. Espinoza with this email?

a. Today's *Daily News*.
b. A copy of his resume.
c. A copy of his degree.
d. A map of Europe.

44

44 Earth Day

We hear the phrase every year, but what exactly is Earth Day? It's an annual event held on April 22nd to focus attention on the environment and how humans influence it. Now observed in nearly 200 countries, it began in 1970 as a day designed to teach American students about the importance of conservation. Over the next 20 years the event was almost forgotten, but it came back in a big way.

» Earth Day 2007 at San Diego City College in San Diego, California (cc by Johntex)

Questions

_____ **1.** What is the writer trying to teach readers about?

a. Communism. **b.** The importance of conservation.
c. Leonardo DiCaprio. **d.** The history of Earth Day.

_____ **2.** When was the first Earth Day observed?

a. In 1870. **b.** In 1970.
c. In 1990. **d.** In 2000.

_____ **3.** Where did Earth Day start?

a. In 141 countries. **b.** In 183 countries.
c. In the Soviet Union. **d.** In the United States.

1990's "Earth Day 20" brought together over 200 million people in 141 countries. It made governments around the world realize the importance of recycling, and put the environment on **the international stage**. It also saw Earth Day become an annual event, rather than one held every ten years. Earth Day 2000 was even bigger, with over 5,000 groups in 183 countries taking part. The Internet was now the event's main organizing tool, and film star Leonardo DiCaprio was its host.

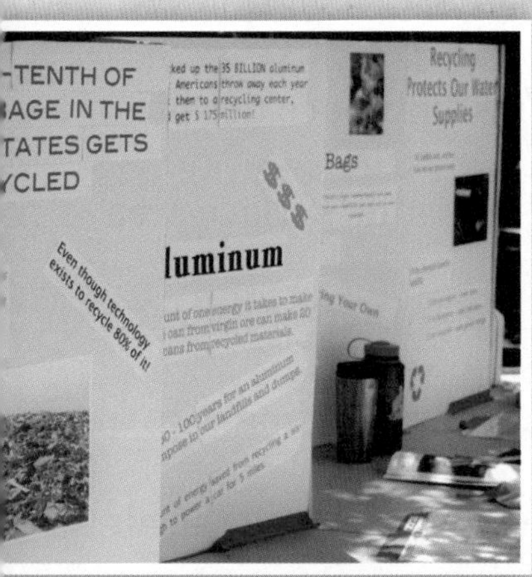

Some believe the choice of April 22nd as Earth Day shows Communist influence. April 22nd, 1970 was the 100th birthday of Soviet leader Vladimir Lenin. The event certainly goes beyond politics now, though, and is a rare example of international agreement.

_____ 4. What is "**the international stage**"?

a. A place where plays from different countries are put on.

b. A place where people from different countries meet.

c. Government and media attention around the world.

d. Agreement among people around the world.

_____ 5. How often is Earth Day observed?

a. Every year.

b. Every 10 years.

c. Every 100 years.

d. It has only been observed three times.

45 Half Man, Half Bird

« A jumper in a wingsuit jumps off a cliff in Norway.

» wingsuit jumper

45

The latest craze in extreme sports has bridged the gap between man and bird. It's called wingsuit flying, and it might just be the most dangerous sport in the world.

Wingsuit flying is a type of BASE jumping, which means people jump off high objects and land with parachutes. The difference lies in the gear involved. A wingsuit jumper wears a suit that adds surface area between his or her arms and legs. This added surface area creates drag, which allows the jumper to fly for several minutes before landing with a parachute. Wingsuit jumpers look very distinctive flying through the air. Some people say they look like bats, and others like superheroes racing to save the day.

As with any other extreme sport, people are **drawn** to wingsuit flying for the thrill of it. However, it can be a very dangerous sport. There's **no room for error** when learning to fly in a wingsuit. One wrong move can mean death, just as it did for Dean Potter, one of the sport's leading figures. Dean died in May 2015 during a jump in Yosemite National Park in the United States.

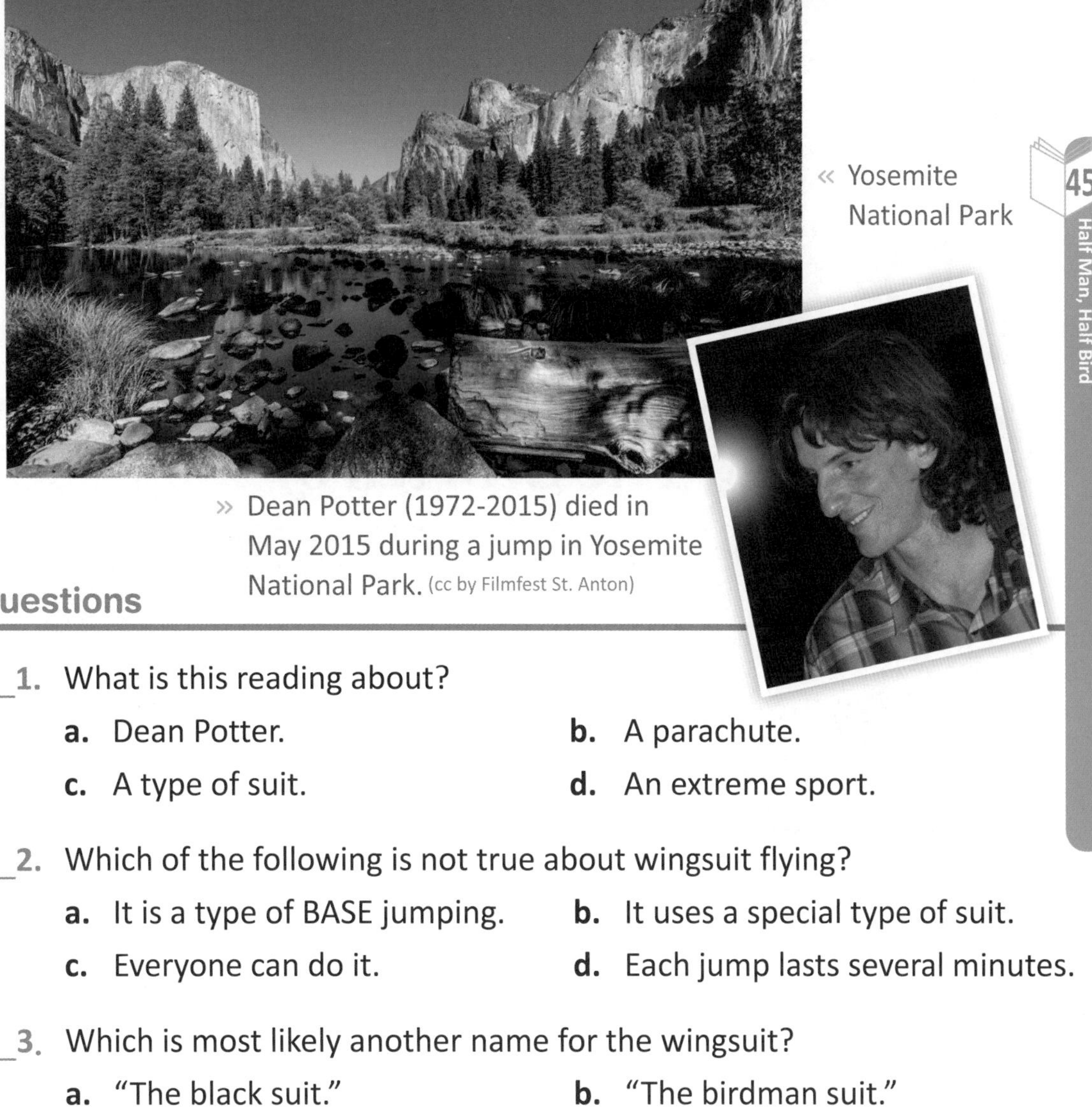

« Yosemite National Park

» Dean Potter (1972-2015) died in May 2015 during a jump in Yosemite National Park. (cc by Filmfest St. Anton)

Questions

_____ 1. What is this reading about?
- a. Dean Potter.
- b. A parachute.
- c. A type of suit.
- d. An extreme sport.

_____ 2. Which of the following is not true about wingsuit flying?
- a. It is a type of BASE jumping.
- b. It uses a special type of suit.
- c. Everyone can do it.
- d. Each jump lasts several minutes.

_____ 3. Which is most likely another name for the wingsuit?
- a. "The black suit."
- b. "The birdman suit."
- c. "The rain suit."
- d. "The Yosemite suit."

_____ 4. Which of the following sentences uses "**draw**" in the same way as the reading?
- a. He likes to draw with colored pencils.
- b. The man in black was the first to draw his gun.
- c. She went upstairs to draw a bath.
- d. The blue door draws attention to the house.

_____ 5. What does it mean that there's "**no room for error**" when learning to fly in a wingsuit?
- a. It's not too hard to figure out how to do it.
- b. One little mistake could mean death.
- c. You should practice inside your house.
- d. It's very easy to make mistakes.

46 Buying a Book Online

The Stories of Ancient Greece

by

Michael Trent and

Maude Lamb

Average Score ★★★★

Buy Now

Quantity 1

E-book $10.99

Paperback $12.99

Add to Basket

The stories of ancient Greece are some of the greatest and most exciting in history. They are stories of love, war, and magic, of jealous gods and brave heroes. These **timeless tales** have been entertaining people for thousands of years, and have influenced some of the Western world's greatest writers.

In this new book by Michael Trent you'll find the stories of monster-killers like Theseus, Perseus, Bellerophon, and Hercules. You'll find sad stories like those of the lovers Pyramus and Thisbe and Orpheus and Eurydice. You'll read about the great warriors of the Trojan War—Achilles, Hector, and Odysseus—and, of course, many, many more.

Trent retells these ancient tales in lively and dramatic language, making them accessible to twenty-first-century readers.

The stories are further **brought to life** by a series of beautiful drawings and paintings by the artist Maude Lamb.

« monster-killer Hercules

Questions

_____1. What is the person reading this thinking about doing?

a. Selling a book.
b. Writing a book.
c. Copying a book.
d. Buying a book.

_____2. Which of these is true about the book?

a. It's set in modern times.
b. Everything in the book really happened.
c. It contains many different stories.
d. It's written in an old-fashioned style.

sculpture of Achilles

_____3. If you "**bring (something) to life**," what do you do?

a. You make it less frightening.
b. You make it more exciting and interesting.
c. You add lots of jokes to it.
d. You make it dull and boring.

_____4. Which of the following can you guess about the book?

a. Most people enjoyed reading it.
b. Not many people bought it.
c. It's expensive compared with other books.
d. There's only one left.

_____5. What are "**timeless tales**"?

a. Stories that are set in the future.
b. Stories that stay popular over the ages.
c. Stories that people used to like but don't anymore.
d. Stories that you can read very quickly.

47 The Glowing Mountain

47

The community of Dasyueshan (Great Snow Mountain) in Taichung City is known for its delicious fruit and beautiful tung flowers. But there's another sight that has people coming to Dasyueshan from all over Taiwan—fireflies.

Great Snow Mountain
(cc by 阿爾特斯)

May is firefly **season** in Dasyueshan. When the sun goes down, the mountainside is blanketed with little floating orbs of warm light. It is a breathtaking sight, and one that brings thousands of tourists to this small aboriginal community every year. These tourists are an economic helping hand to the people of Dasyueshan, who are still recovering from the Jiji earthquake.

tung flower
(cc by Hslung/ d6478coke)

Questions

_____ 1. What is this reading trying to say?
- a. People should not view fireflies.
- b. Fireflies are disappearing all over Taiwan.
- c. We should be responsible when viewing fireflies.
- d. Dasyueshan was hit hard by the Jiji earthquake.

_____ 2. Which of the following is not one of the "**five nos**"?
- a. No watching them.
- b. No chasing them.
- c. No loud noises.
- d. No lights.

_____ 3. What does it mean if something is "**off-limits**"?
- a. It's turned on.
- b. It's not allowed.
- c. It's very rare.
- d. It's hard to see.

« Taichung City

» fireflies

Dasyueshan is a good example of the link between the natural environment and local livelihoods. Efforts are being made to protect this environment and make sure that tourists don't cause any damage. Lights are turned off throughout the community during firefly **season**. Even car headlights are **off-limits**. Tourists must park their cars and walk the final 1,300 meters to the viewing area. When viewing fireflies, tourists are asked to follow the "**five nos**." These are: no chasing them, no catching them, no getting close to their homes, no loud noises, and no lights.

^ Jiji

______ **4.** Which of the following sentences uses "**season**" in the same way as the reading?

a. The apples are in season right now.
b. Winter is the coldest season in Canada.
c. The television show ran for three seasons.
d. The basketball season is almost over.

______ **5.** Which of the following statements is most likely true?

a. Motorcycles are allowed in the firefly viewing area.
b. The Jiji earthquake hurt businesses in Dasyueshan.
c. There are no lights in the entire community of Dasyueshan.
d. Daytime is the best time to view fireflies in Dasyueshan.

48 Breathable Roads

Chen Jui Wen on magazine cover

Most scientists agree that weather will become more unpredictable in the years ahead. That means more storms, flooding, and droughts all over the planet. Luckily for us, there are people who are already developing fresh ways to **make the most** of the new normal.

Chen Jui Wen is one such person. He invented JW permeable pavement, which is a road that can absorb water like a sponge. When water touches this "breathable road," it is absorbed by little plastic tubes. The water is then cleaned by a layer of rocks and kept in a large tank for future use. This means rain can be collected and stored for when the weather gets too dry.

The benefits don't end there. JW permeable pavement can also absorb heat, stop snow from piling up, and even clean up air pollution. And it doesn't need a lot of special maintenance.

Breathable roads have already been built in Taipei's Xizhi District and lots of other places. Chen Jui Wen believes they will soon **catch on** all over the world. They might not save money in the short term, but they can save a lot by preventing costly floods over the long term.

Taiwanese inventor Chen Jui Wen (by PING TAI CO., LTD.)

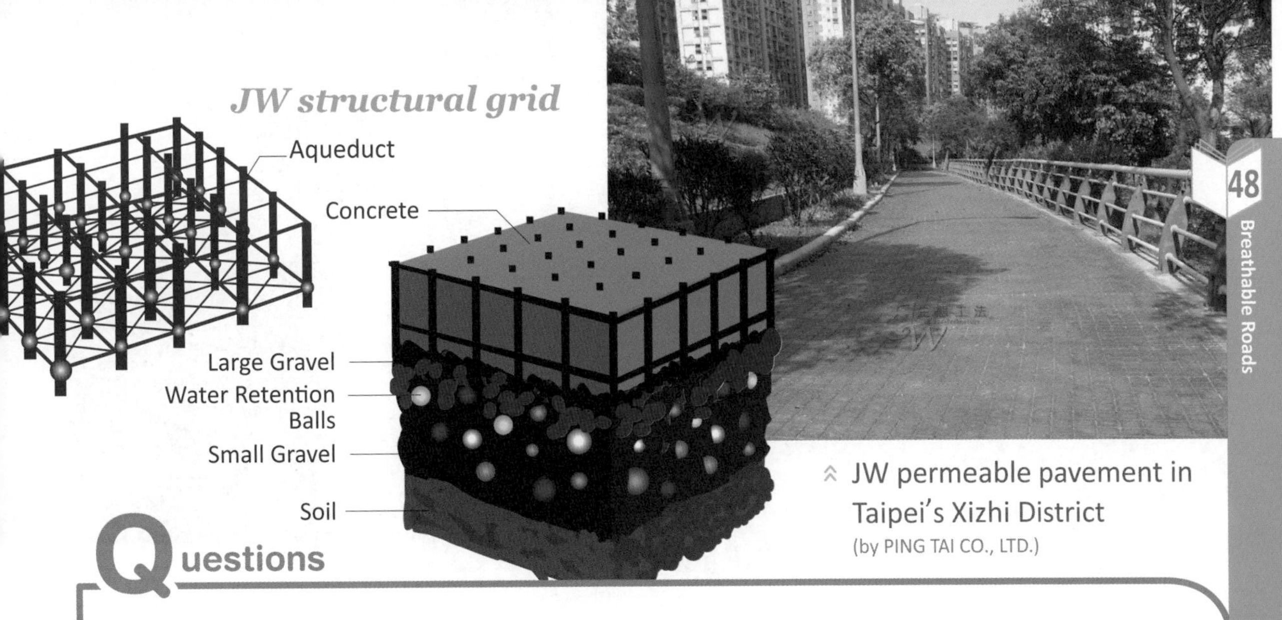

JW permeable pavement in Taipei's Xizhi District
(by PING TAI CO., LTD.)

Questions

_____ 1. What is this reading about?

a. Chen Jui Wen. b. JW permeable pavement.
c. Taipei's Xizhi District. d. Droughts.

_____ 2. Which of the following is not one of the breathing road's functions?

a. Cleaning water. b. Stopping noise pollution.
c. Storing water. d. Cleaning the air.

_____ 3. What does it mean to "**make the most**" of a situation?

a. To do your best in a bad situation.
b. To try to make as much money as possible.
c. To learn new skills from a good situation.
d. To turn a good situation into a bad situation.

_____ 4. Which of the following is most likely true about breathable roads?

a. They are more expensive than regular roads.
b. They can be used to charge your smartphone.
c. They can prevent all car crashes.
d. Children aren't allowed to walk on them.

_____ 5. What does it mean that Chen Jui Wen believes breathable roads will "**catch on**" all over the world?

a. People will come from everywhere to see them.
b. They will be built everywhere.
c. People everywhere will hear about them.
d. They will soon be forgotten.

» Trojan Horse in Troy, Turkey

≈ In computing, a Trojan horse is a type of computer virus.

49 The Trojan Horse

Viruses, worms, Trojan horses—all of these are programs that can do serious damage to your computer. Trojan horses are particularly difficult to avoid, as they seem perfectly harmless at first. A Trojan horse might **disguise** itself as an email attachment or a fun-looking download. Then, when it's inside your computer, it steals all your personal data or deletes all your files.

But where does the term **Trojan horse** come from? A long time ago, a war is said to have been fought between Greece and the city of Troy. The wall around the city was so high and strong that the Greeks just couldn't get inside. After 10 years of war, the Greeks finally came up with a plan. They built a huge wooden horse and hid soldiers inside it. Then they pretended to sail home. The Trojans, thinking they had won the war, took the horse inside their city walls to celebrate their victory. That night, the soldiers inside the horse jumped out and opened the city gates. The rest of the Greek army, which had sailed back to Troy secretly in the night, entered the city and destroyed it.

« Troy

Questions

_____ 1. What is the writer trying to teach readers about?

a. Ancient Greek culture. b. The dangers of the Internet.
c. The source of a phrase. d. The history of cheating.

_____ 2. How did the wooden horse help the Greeks win the war against Troy?

a. It scared the Trojans away.
b. It brought them good luck.
c. It inspired them to fight harder.
d. It got them inside Troy's city walls.

_____ 3. What does "**disguise**" most likely mean?

a. Kill. b. Trick. c. Hide. d. Win.

_____ 4. Why did the Greeks sail away from Troy?

a. They wanted the Trojans to chase them.
b. They wanted the Trojans to think they'd won.
c. They wanted to watch the Trojans secretly.
d. They wanted to keep their ships safe.

_____ 5. Which of these could also be described as a "**Trojan horse**"?

a. A false friend. b. A difficult test.
c. A brave soldier. d. An old story.

« Greece

50

50 Bike Thief Notice

ATTENTION

There have been several bike thefts reported in our community over the past three weeks. The first one took place on the corner of Charleston Road and Fleet Street, where four bikes were stolen. The most recent one occurred just last weekend, when a bike was stolen out of a garage on Madison Road.

We have two reasons to believe that these thefts are connected. For one, we know that bike thefts were **unheard** of within the gates of our peaceful community. To have a sudden rash of them like this indicates the work of one "**bad apple**." There have also been witnesses to some of the thefts.

Questions

_____ 1. What is this article about?

a. A community. **b.** Four bikes. **c.** Security guards. **d.** A thief.

_____ 2. Which of the following is not true about the suspect?

a. He is a male.
b. People have seen him stealing bikes.
c. He wears sunglasses.
d. He likes to dress in colorful clothing.

_____ 3. What is a "**bad apple**"?

a. Someone who loves eating fruit.
b. Someone who breaks the rules.
c. Someone who has many friends.
d. Someone who has no money.

community

security guard

thief

If you see someone who looks like this, please call the community association or the police right away. We are serious about catching this thief, and someone will be manning the hotline 24 hours a day. Regular security patrols of the community will also be on the lookout. A drawing of the suspect has been provided to each of our security guards.

These witnesses have described the following suspect:

- **Male, around 180 cm tall**
- **Shoulder-length black hair**
- **"Reddish skin on his face," said one witness**
- **Last seen wearing black jeans, a black sweatshirt, and sunglasses**

_____ **4.** Which of the following is likely a duty of the community association?

a. Maintaining law and order in the community.
b. Providing bikes to members of the community.
c. Building the houses in the community.
d. Providing jobs to members of the community.

_____ **5.** What does it mean that bike thefts were "**unheard of**"?

a. They never happened.
b. They didn't make any noise.
c. They were serious crimes.
d. They were talked about by everyone.

TRANSLATION

1 看電影的一天

　　我朋友和我今天想去看電影，我們到便利商店買了一份報紙，電影時刻表就在最後一頁。讓我們來看看今天上映哪些電影。

2 好朋友的定義

迪娜：我還是不敢相信，我才和前男友分手不久，塔拉那麼快就和他約會。

麗莎：我相信，她一直是只在乎自己的自私鬼。老實說，我不懂妳為什麼還和她當朋友，她完全不管妳快不快樂。

迪娜：哇，妳跟我媽講的簡直如出一轍，她總是跟我說，好朋友會以同理心互相關心。

麗莎：她說的沒錯。而且，妳們兩個完全沒有交集，妳是力爭上游的好學生……

迪娜：……她寧願把心思放在血拼和交男朋友。

麗莎：還記得上次她在妳應該要唸書的時候，說服妳幫她找一件完美的新洋裝嗎？

迪娜：當然記得，那次考試我考不及格，很氣自己。

麗莎：是不是？她連妳的需求都不在乎。如果我是妳，就會和她絕交。

迪娜：妳說得對，這段友誼沒有建設性，我的人生中需要多一點像妳這樣的朋友，謝謝妳說出真心話。

麗莎：誰叫我們是好朋友！

3 英文討論區

Maria132

14:15，Maria132的留言：

嗨，大家好：

我的英文老師出了一個問題當作業，但我不曉得答案是什麼，有人能幫我嗎？

On Mondays, I'm usually at work until/since 7 p.m.

（每逢星期一，我通常會上班至／從晚上7點）

請問哪一個才正確？拜託幫幫忙！

謝謝囉。 瑪麗亞

RedHarry67

14:30，RedHarry67 回覆：

正確答案是until。since的用法在於敘述仍進行中的某件事於何時開始。

（例如，我現在在上班，我從早上7點工作到現在）

until的用法則是敘述某件事的結束時間。

（例如，我早上7點開始上班，直到晚上7點才能下班）。

希望對妳有幫助！ 哈利

KipJones21

14:42，KipJones21 回覆：

妳應該可以從句子的時態找出答案。

句子裡有since的時候，我們通常會用現在完成式（have/has + 過去分詞）或現在完成進行式（have/has been + -ing）。如果句子是「I have been at work until/since 7 p.m.」，那麼正確答案就是since。但妳的句子是用簡單現在式來描述例行事務（I'm usually at work . . . ），所以不可能用since。

奇普

Maria132

14:50，Maria132 回覆：

感謝奇普和哈利你們的幫忙！

經過你們一解釋，真的清楚多了！:)

4 安全返家

蘇：嗨，老媽！我放學後可以去茱莉家嗎？她剛養了一隻小倉鼠，我想去瞧瞧。

老媽：親愛的，今天不行，我不希望妳走夜路回家。

蘇：別這麼老古板嘛，老媽，我可以走夜路回家。

老媽：想都別想！

蘇：但是明蒂的爸媽都讓她在外面待到晚上9點才回家。

老媽：那妳可以搬去和明蒂的爸媽住，我想他們不會介意的。

蘇：拜託，這一次就好！我保證我會洗碗洗一個星期。

老媽：那史密斯老師的課交代的簡報呢？就是關於第二次世界大戰起因的那項功課。

蘇：我兩個禮拜前就做完了。

老媽：好吧，你可以在茱莉家待到晚上7點，然後晚一點吃晚餐。

蘇：萬歲！我的傍晚行程有救了。

老媽：既然我很老古板，妳應該知道我接下來要說什麼，對吧？

蘇：妳要講「親愛的，看完就趕快回家，不要跟任何陌生人說話」之類的。

老媽：不用我講就好。

9月1日

我今天又在桌上發現一張紙條，署名「愛慕妳的人」，希望不是吉姆寫的。

9月5日

我已經受夠了受訓這件事，我才不在乎十一月的兩項大活動，教練怎能期望我每兩天跑10公里？算了，這傢伙根本是機器人，他會這樣想一點也不意外，我不指望他能了解人類也是會痛的。

9月7日

吉姆終於鼓起勇氣，在下課後找我講話，他問我是否能加他為臉書好友，我告訴他，我並沒有臉書帳號，從他的表情看來，我想他不相信我。

9月13日

將近一個星期都沒有任何新紙條，看來「愛慕我的人」終於懂我的意思了。

9月15日

吉姆竟然和莎拉出去！怎麼會這樣？她是校花耶，看來吉姆這個人真是不可貌相，我居然斷送了和他發展的機會……

6 課後才藝班

我這個年級的很多學生，放學後都會再去上課。有的是補習班，能協助學生在數學或英文等特定科目表現更好；有的是才藝班，例如舞蹈課或學習某樂器的音樂課。我覺得自然科學很難，所以我媽讓我每星期三都去補習，我每星期二放學後還會去上鋼琴課。我想知道和我同年級的其他學生，有多少人和我差不多，所以我做了一份問卷調查，並將結果製成以下圖表。

7 相愛與離婚

蔓維斯

親愛的蔓維斯：

我今年15歲，我擔心爸媽快離婚了。爭吵不是主要因素，因為自我有印象以來，他們一直吵個不停。讓我無法忍受的是他們的漠不關心。有時我們一起吃晚餐，全程鴉雀無聲，他們根本不像夫妻，兩個人似乎都不在乎對方的想法或感受，這樣一點都不正常，是吧？謝謝妳傾聽我的問題，長久以來，我一直是妳的忠實讀者兼粉絲。 約翰

親愛的約翰：

看來你們家正經歷一段難熬的過程。我不敢說你的父母會不會離婚，但你一定要記住，不管發生什麼事，他們依然愛你。我們還小的時候，會覺得父母都知道自己在做什麼，其實不一定。你的爸媽可能還很心煩意亂，不曉得接下來該怎麼做，所以他們會出現一些不尋常的行為。

希望我的回覆幫得上忙。 蔓維斯

8 薪資門檻多低才能過關？

勞工可領取到的報酬最小值，稱為最低薪資。此數字舉足輕重，因為攸關全球上百萬名勞工的生活品質。

每個國家均制定不同的最低薪資標準。政客依據生活水準來訂定，也就是以「勞工需要多少薪資才能讓生活收支打平」來衡量。問題是情況會不斷變動，有時飲食、汽油和租金等開銷上漲，但最低薪資仍停滯不變，對勞工來說，實在苦不堪言。

政客避免調升最低薪資的原因，在於他們認為不利於企業，因為資方必須向勞方支付更多費用。但是，許多人不認同此看法，因為最低薪資提高，表示每個人的可支配金額變多，因此消費能力變好而能促進經濟發展。

9 我最大的恐懼

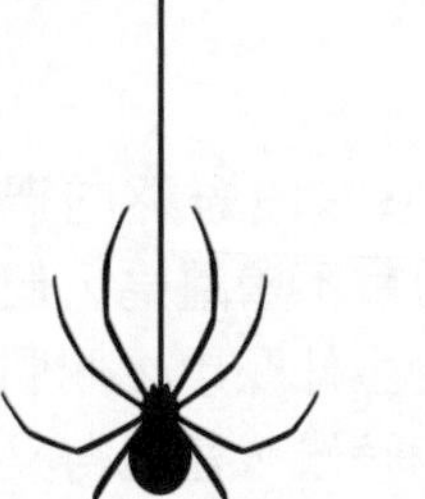

我不怕蜘蛛或蛇，

或是躲在床底下的怪物，

我不信世上有鬼或巫婆、

吸血鬼、狼人或活屍。

我天不怕地不怕，也不怕黑，

我還覺得老鼠很可愛，甚至願意和鯊魚悠游於海洋。

那我到底怕什麼？

我做了一個夢，

夜復一夜不斷出現，

夢裡的我，早上醒來發現，

這世界空無一人——只有我還存在。

空蕩蕩的街道和房子，電視上連個人影也沒有。

我想，也許大家都丟下我，跑去另一個世界。

他們心想：把這煩人的女孩留在這吧。

我得自言自語，剛開始還無妨，

過了一陣子，

你會發現世上最糟的事，

就是一而再、再而三的聽相同的故事，

還沒有人和你一起編織新內容，

到最後我發瘋了！我孤單一人，自力更生，

這也許就是我最害怕的事……

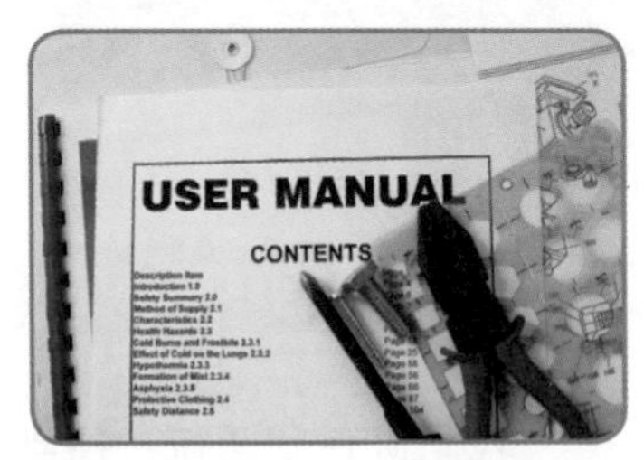

10 組裝說明

親愛的辛蒂：

別擔心！很多人跟您一樣，不知道如何組裝我們派瑞莫型號的產品。我很樂意一步一步指導您。組裝步驟如下：

1. 請先清點組裝用的零組件，應該要有四支桌腳、四個金屬支架、上下層板、四個塑膠桌腳套，以及十六個螺絲。
2. 先將塑膠桌腳套套上桌腳。
3. 確認好上層板的底部是哪一面，底部應有可栓進螺絲的孔洞，然後將金屬支架栓於上層板底部，每個支架需使用四個螺絲。
4. 將四支桌腳分別滑入金屬支架，因為桌腳已套入四個塑膠腳套，因此已能自行直立。
5. 將下層板滑入上層板底面，讓四支桌腳固定住下層板。

如果您想充分運用派瑞莫，我們建議您粉刷上層板，即可防止桌面因為經年累月用餐而磨損。

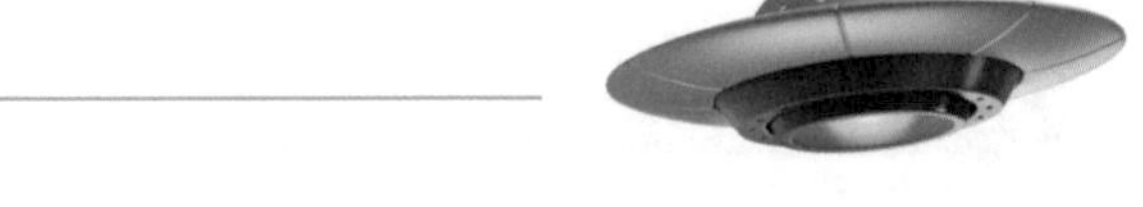

11 她與眾不同

我和這個女孩已經約會一陣子，
本來以為她是我的真命天女，
但最近我察覺到不尋常的怪事，
或許你聽了也會認同。

她拿下眼鏡，盯著我看的，
是一對銀色的大眼睛，
她的頭髮不自然，經常脫落。
老天，這真的是出人意外，
這個女孩不太對勁，
因為她雙腿遍佈紫色腳毛……

[副歌]
我的女友不正常，
雖然很可愛，但我覺得她是外星人。
我媽說這不過是青春期的現象，
但她的皮膚卻發綠呀，發綠呀……

我發現她對著外觀奇特的手機低語，
說著我聽不懂的語言，
我想她可能在和遙遠飛碟上的人通話。

這個女孩不太對勁，
因為她的耳朵長得太尖了……
[副歌]
這個女孩不太對勁——因為她的全名是
賽賽巴勒。
[副歌]

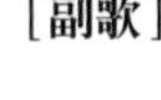

12 3B 班的午茶時間

我們班有個傳統，每到午餐時間，大家都會去附近的茶店買些茶飲。本來一直都只有「吉兒茶館」和「饗茶」兩間茶店，但到了四月底，我聽說五月初會新開一家「只有為你」茶館。我很好奇，新開張的競爭者會如何影響其他店家？還有，我的同學們會想去哪一家捧場？大家會忠於原味還是嚐鮮呢？所以，整整五月份的午餐時間，我都會詢問大家買了哪一家的茶飲，並將結果製成下表。

13 什麼樣的工作適合你？

請進行線上測驗，瞭解適合自己的工作。

請瀏覽以下活動／主題，勾選您有興趣的部分，以及喜愛的程度，然後按下「提交」，即可顯示我們針對您的個性所篩選出的合適工作名單。

 **沒興趣**

 **非常有興趣**

運動、養生等等	銷售
收集資料	體力活 （園藝、營建、修繕等等）
使顧客滿意	文書或影像處理
發想新點子	負責領導團體
幫助他人學習新技能	與兒童或青少年一同工作
幫助他人相處愉快	

提交

14 追思派特阿姨

派翠西亞・莎拉・史密斯於週一深夜病逝於博爾頓紀念醫院。臨終前，親朋好友都陪在身邊，長期對抗病魔的她，在睡夢中安詳辭世，享年75歲。

家人暱稱為「派特阿姨」的派翠西亞，走過精采的一生。當年來到哈里法克斯的她，還只是個嬰兒，從小就認識她的人，都會異口同聲的說，派翠西亞非常頑皮。她從不愛玩洋娃娃或扮家家酒，爬樹和打籃球才是她的拿手絕活。

直到她遇見亞瑟，才開始安定下來。亞瑟對派特無微不至，即使在學校，也堅持幫派特拿書。他們結褵40年且育有三子女，兩人的愛情火花，仍如第一天相識般那樣地熾熱，他們在各方面都是十分契合的心靈伴侶。

我們會懷念她，但不應哀悼她的逝去，而是讚頌她經歷了愛與幸福的長久人生。

15 來打球吧！

我超愛棒球，這是我最愛的運動。中華職業棒球大聯盟只有四支球隊在比賽，和美國職棒大聯盟的38支球隊相較下並不多。不過，每支球隊一年的例行賽事有120場，因此，要記錄勝場（W）、平手（T）、敗場（L）的次數不容易，所以球季期間，各隊分數都會記入表格。以下就是本年度球季結束後的職棒聯盟戰績表。

16 何謂莓果？

我敢說，大家一定不知道草莓竟然不是一種莓果，覆盆莓和黑莓也不屬於莓果。上述所謂的「莓類」水果皆為複合果，意思是從花朵中的數個子房發育而成。而真正的莓果屬於單果，也就是從一朵花的單一子房發育出來。

花朵授粉後，子房部分就會生長出果實，有些花卉僅有單一子房，有些花卉則有許多子房。果實必須從僅有單一子房的花朵中形成，才可謂莓果，也就是說，葡萄、香蕉、番茄甚至是西瓜等果實，均可稱為莓果。反而有許多所謂的莓類水果不是莓果。事實上，草莓表面看似細小的「種籽」，根本不是種籽，而是草莓開花後含有種籽的子房，這麼多的子房真是數也數不清！

大家將複合果稱為「莓果」，卻將真正的莓果命名為其他稱呼，這樣的現象從何而來不得而知，即使我們仍將錯就錯，至少現在我們已經清楚從市場買回來的水果該歸類為何種果實了。

17 足球實況報導

……威廉斯接到球了，他把球傳給麥克斯。麥克斯因腳踝嚴重受傷休息了六個月，最近才剛回到中城聯盟隊，很開心看到他恢復健康歸隊。他試著突破重圍——喔！居然被彼得斯鏟球，這球鏟得漂亮。現在球到了彼得斯腳上，他不停奔跑，越過丹尼爾斯。蓋瑞想鏟彼得斯的球，但他閃過去了！竟然打敗兩個後衛，現在他和守門員之間空無一人，彼得斯起腳射球！進球得分！柏林翰城隊又得一分，形成領先的局面。時間只剩三分鐘，比數2比1。我想柏林翰城隊會贏球，因為以中城聯盟隊下半場攻略狀態來看，很難再得分。柏林翰城隊的後衛超強，而中城聯盟隊在上半場快結束時踢進的那一球，可說是他們整場球賽中最厲害的表現，接下來就一直處於不利情勢。不過，剩最後幾分鐘，我們還是靜觀其變看看……

18 魔術技法：教學影片

大家好，歡迎再次觀賞《邁克的魔術講堂》。今天，我要教大家變的魔術叫做「硬幣穿透玻璃」。

首先，我示範一下。

我的左手拿著一個小玻璃碗，右手拿著一個硬幣。現在我將硬幣放在右手手心，然後用手掌輕打碗底下方一次、兩次、三次，看吧！硬幣穿透碗底，跑到碗裡面了。

現在我們來解密這個魔術。

首先，一定要像這樣以大拇指和中指拿住碗口的部分，然後在手心輕打碗底下方第二次時，悄悄地將硬幣從手心移到指尖，像這樣做。最後一次用手心輕打碗底時，讓左手指尖的硬幣順勢掉入碗內，看起來就像是從碗底下方穿透至碗內。

大家切記喔，熟能生巧，所以別擔心無法快速上手。下次見囉！

19 作家的摯友

寫作是一件很棒的事，但寫作能力的養成卻不易，不僅需要時間勤奮練習，還要運用一些外來助力才能得心應手，這就是寫作有趣的地方。你可以閱讀上百本如何成為好作家的工具書，卻不一定有所助益。精進寫作技巧的最佳方法，就是閱讀任何唾手可得的書籍，才能吸收不同的寫作與敘事風格。最重要的是好好練習，寫得越多，越能游刃有餘。

加拿大籍女作家加布莉爾・洛伊曾提及：「沒有藝術的幫助下，我們該如何了解對方的一絲一毫？」她說的有道理。因此，趕緊提筆，讓世人見識你的才華。

寫作入門指南

目錄

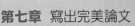

第一章 好文章的影響力

第二章 工欲善其事，必先利其器

第三章 良好的寫作環境

第四章 文法與造句

第五章 名人對寫作的看法

第六章 句子的重要性

第七章 寫出完美論文

第八章 寫出動人故事

第九章 寫詩

第十章 商業文書

20 短篇小說比賽

徵文活動！

你覺得自己寫的小說能拔得頭籌嗎？馬上參加第17屆新城圖書館年度短篇小說比賽，就有機會贏得獎金1000元。前三名得主的作品還能發表於《新城時報》。

獎品

第一名：1000元支票，作品將刊登於《新城時報》。

第二名：作品將刊登於《新城時報》，以及300元的圖書禮券。

第三名：作品將刊登於《新城時報》，以及150元的圖書禮券。

參加辦法

請將作品郵寄至新城公立圖書館（地址為新城市高街45號），或是親自前來圖書館交件，而且參賽作品數量不限！

- 作品請以Times New Roman字型、字體大小為12的格式打於電子檔，再列印於白底的A4紙張交出。我們不接受手寫稿件。
- 每篇小說的字數上限為2000字。
- 請於稿件第一頁附上您的全名與聯絡資料。

務必繳交出自本人創作且尚未出版的作品。

我們期待拜讀您的大作！

21 黑色黃金

大家是否曾想過，石油為何號稱「黑色黃金」？原因在於石油的用途廣泛！我們可利用石油發動汽車或供應居家暖氣，甚至能在洗髮乳和牙膏等生活用品中發現石油成分的蹤跡。

石油如此實用，也難怪各國政府總是聞油價色變。表面上，油價看似簡單的計算結果，也就是取決於供需狀態。供大於需，油價就會下跌；供不應求，油價就會上漲。但其實沒有這麼單純，油價還會取決於時事，意思就是只要產油國稍有爆發戰爭的跡象，油價就會飆漲。

22 韓國保寧美容泥漿節

七月準備好去哪兒玩了嗎？如果尚無頭緒，何不參加保寧美容泥漿節？距離首爾不到200公里，從7月17日至26日，將有上百萬人湧進大川海水浴場同歡保寧美容泥漿節。

參加對象

保寧這座小鎮，每年此刻的人口都會從十萬人左右爆增為上百萬人，韓國人、外籍工作者與國外遊客齊聚一堂，慶祝此知名的世界慶典。無論你來自何方，歡迎盡情放鬆，享受泥漿帶來的樂趣！

為何舉辦泥漿節？

保寧泥漿有益肌膚與身體健康，更有研究證明的加持。事實上，第一屆美容泥漿節於1998年開辦，目的在於讓大家更加了解保寧泥漿類美妝產品，活動盛況空前，因此衍生為年度慶典。

活動內容

- 泥漿滑水道
- 臉部泥漿彩繪
- 泥漿浴
- 現場音樂表演
- 煙火（僅於深夜開放）
- 泥漿美妝產品

別再猶豫！
馬上安排一窺保寧美景的行程！

23 租借自行車

感謝您對iBike系統的支持！您可以使用捷運卡租借自行車，並於市內任一租借站歸還。首先，請將捷運卡置於以下讀卡機。如有問題，請參閱以下說明。

錯誤代碼	訊息	解決辦法
0	**無法讀卡**	請再試一次。如仍有問題，請試讀另一張卡片。
1	**此卡尚未註冊**	請至距離最近的iBike電腦螢幕註冊您的卡片。
2	**此卡已有人使用**	目前已有其他人正在使用此卡片，若您剛歸還iBike，請稍等兩分鐘後再試一次。
3	**卡片儲值額度不足**	您的卡片儲值金額不足，請儲值後再試一次。
4	**卡片不符**	租借iBike的卡片與歸還iBike的卡片不符，請使用另一張卡片。
5	**本機服務暫停**	iBike系統目前停用中，請稍候片刻再試一次，抱歉造成您的不便。

24 潔牙方式的古往今來

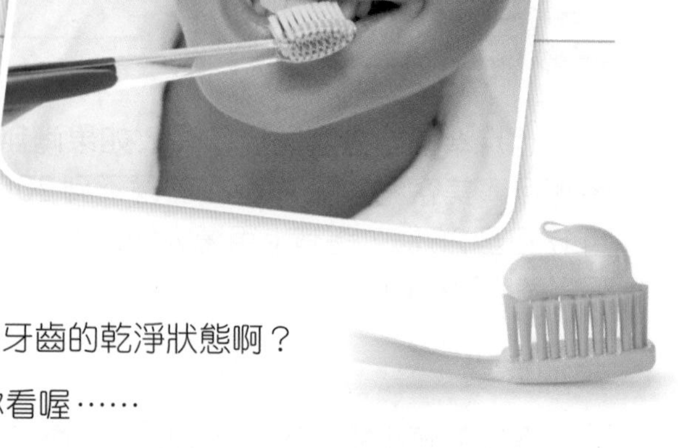

媽媽：珍妮，睡覺前別忘了刷牙好嗎？

珍妮：我會記得……對了，老媽？

媽媽：怎麼啦？

珍妮：牙刷和牙膏發明之前，人類怎麼保持牙齒的乾淨狀態啊？

媽媽：問得好。我們何不一起上網查查？妳看喔……

珍妮：好。這個網站說，牙刷發明之前，人類用粗布或棍子潔牙。即使是現在，中東和非洲的某些民族，仍用小棍子潔牙，他們會將棍子折斷，用斷口的那一端摩擦牙齒！

媽媽：那他們用什麼東西代替牙膏呢？

珍妮：很多不同的東西，例如香料、鹽巴、白土粉、灰燼……不過網站也說，以前的飲食習慣糖分偏低，所以古人不太需要過於悉心照料牙齒。

媽媽：有意思。而且，目前仍有些生活方式傳統的民族幾乎不用刷牙，因為他們根本不吃西方食物！所以妳得到想要的解答了嗎？

珍妮：得到啦！謝了老媽，晚安。

25 動物王國的母性光輝

親愛的日記：

今天上學十分有趣，因為適逢母親節，很多堂課都以母親節為上課主題。我們從歷史課得知母親節的歷史；社會課告訴我們不同文化的母親節概況；英文課則學到和母親節有關的詩句，但我今天最喜歡生物課。

我們瞭解到動物王國的母性光輝，有些動物媽媽真的是為母則強！例如某些深海章魚能捍衛自己的卵囊超過四年的時間，這期間還幾乎不吃不喝。有的鯊魚（應該是皺鰓鯊）孕期甚至長達三年半！我跟媽說這件事，她回「好險不是我！」我也跟媽說蠍子媽媽的事，蠍子媽媽產後，會一直揹著寶寶直到長大為止。媽說她有時覺得自己像蠍子，因為她也總是開車載著我和姊妹們到處跑！不過我之後送她一盒巧克力和卡片，看得出來她蠻開心的。

好吧，該睡覺了。
晚安囉，日記！

26 辨別說謊的表情

如果你說自己從未說過謊，其實就是在說謊。事實上，以談話10分鐘來看，多數人至少會說一次謊。也許說謊的用意在於保護某人，或想讓某人免於尷尬；也有可能是為了一己之私扯謊，好讓自己佔上風。無論說謊的動機是善意或惡意，我們都會說謊。

那麼，我們該如何辨別真偽？研究人員已找到能幫助大家察覺謊言蛛絲馬跡的方法（也有可能讓大家變得擅於說謊！）。

- **眼神接觸**——說話時，眼神接觸的頻率過少或過多。
- **過於滔滔不絕**——主動透露太多沒被過問的細節與資訊。
- **重複**——一再說出相同的字眼或話語（例如「不是我，不是我」）。
- **頭部姿勢**——變換頭部姿勢，例如頭歪一邊或歪頭時又擺正。
- **肢體語言**——站著或坐著時動來動去，或是完全不動。
- **摸嘴巴**——被問及某問題時，會摸嘴巴或掩嘴。

27 遊戲玩家概況

世界各地愛打電玩的人或所謂的「遊戲玩家」，可說是越來越普遍。事實上，2013年全球電玩遊戲的銷售額超過930億美元。《俠盜獵車手5》這款電玩甚至在全球賣出3300萬套，銷售額共計20億美元，簡直超越《復仇者聯盟》這類熱門電影，因為票房僅剛好掠過15億美元而已。

全球電玩產業的其中兩種遊戲類別最為蓬勃發展，一個是手機遊戲，也就是使用介面為智慧型手機的電玩。你可能注意過，捷運上的每位乘客都在點滑手機玩遊戲；大型多人線上角色扮演遊戲（MMORPG）則是另一個蒸蒸日上的類別，因為MMORPG建構的線上世界，能容納千百名玩家盡情探索冒險。

28 氣象預報

今天早晨的新聞到此播報完畢，接下來由吉兒為大家播報氣象。

馬丁謝謝你。大家早，今天是5月5日星期五，我是吉兒・龐德，現在為您播報本週末的氣象預報。全國今天的氣候恐怕多為雨天。北部和東北部地區的早上會降下豪雨，下午很有可能延續這樣的情況，直到傍晚才會稍微減緩。西北部地區早上的氣候雖然差不多，但到了下午應該能撥雲見日，稍晚甚至可能出現和煦陽光。不過南部地區的民眾就沒有這麼幸運了，因為猛烈的暴風雨將橫掃南部一整天，傍晚也不例外。

接下來看看明天和週日的氣象，可說是一百八十度大轉變。所有地區在週六和週日都是萬里無雲的晴朗好天氣，一整天均為風和日麗的狀態，氣溫大約是華氏70度——絕對是適合野餐的好氣候！氣象預報到此播報完畢，祝大家有個愉快的週末。

29 每日星座運勢

牡羊座
3月21日—4月19日

你今天會遇見重要的人物，確保你讓人留下良好的第一印象。

金牛座
4月20日—5月20日

請與蓄鬍的人保持距離，因為這類男子可能會對你不利。

雙子座
5月21日—6月20日

你的麻吉在慶祝某盛大事件，別忘了恭喜他，否則可是會失去一位摯友。

天秤座
9月23日—10月22日

你今天將會遇見夢中情人，別讓幸福溜走。

天蠍座
10月23日—11月21日

打通電話給爸媽吧，你一定會慶幸自己這麼做。

射手座
11月22日—12月21日

雖然今天的你身負重責大任，但很有可能凸槌，延到明天再完成吧。

巨蟹座
6月21日—7月22日

今天是嚐鮮的好日子，嘗試一下從未做過的事，好運絕對接踵而來。

獅子座
7月23日—8月22日

今天出門將讓你諸事不順，最好宅在家。

處女座
8月23日—9月22日

你很有可能發生意外，今天請格外小心。

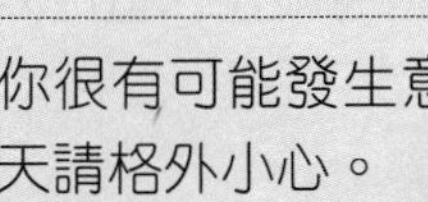

魔羯座
12月22日—1月19日

如果你今天送個小禮給心愛的人，將能讓兩人感情更加升溫。

水瓶座
1月20日—2月18日

今天會有人試圖霸凌你，請為自己挺身而出，你的人生將因此產生重大改變。

雙魚座
2月19日—3月20日

你今天將有機會以眼還眼，請別這麼做，否則後果不堪設想。

晶透亮膚面膜

綠茶配方

「晶透」品牌新推出的此款面膜，含天然綠茶萃取精華，能讓肌膚倍感清新、撫平細紋，同時防止肌膚乾燥。

使用方式：

1 先以香皂與溫水清潔臉部。
2 打開包裝並拿出面膜。
3 撕除面膜背面的底紙。
4 先從額頭部位開始，將面膜往下巴方向敷於臉部。
5 以雙手輕壓面膜，避免未服貼於臉部而產生空隙。
6 等候15 - 20分鐘的時間。
7 取下面膜，按摩臉部，讓肌膚吸收剩餘的面膜精華液。

如需看見最佳保養成效，請一週使用一次或兩次。

注意：

1 肌膚若開始泛紅或覺得刺激，請立刻停止使用本面膜。
2 肌膚若有傷口或敏感刺激問題，請勿使用本面膜。
3 避免直接接觸眼睛。如果出現敏感刺激問題，請以清水立刻沖淨眼睛。

31 蟑螂斷頭後還能存活嗎？

如果你家裡曾出現過蟑螂，你一定知道有多難消滅牠們，有時光是重踩還殺不死，據說蟑螂連核子彈的威力都敵得過。如今，科學家已發現這些神奇小強，斷頭後竟然仍能維持生命！

原因在於蟑螂和人類不同，並非透過口部呼吸，而是以佈滿全身上下的小孔呼吸。此外，與人類相異的另一點，在於蟑螂身體各部位均有微型的腦部器官。也就是說，即使斷頭，蟑螂仍保有感官與四處移動的能力。此外，蟑螂不像人類一樣需要經常進食，只要吃一餐，蟑螂就能維持數週的生命。

雖然斷頭蟑螂早晚都會喪命，但卻能維持這樣的狀態存活數週之久！更奇怪的是，蟑螂頭也能延續生命跡象！蟑螂頭與身體分離後，還能揮動觸鬚達數小時的時間。這樣的特質，或許讓蟑螂成為全地球生命力最強韌的生物！

32 失物招領公告

有人遺失物品嗎？

首先，感謝大家昨晚參加學校的聖誕派對！希望大家都玩得盡興。不過，有些人可能玩得太開心，以至於忘了帶走自己的東西！清潔小組在打掃整理的時候，在學校體育館內與四周發現以下物品：

一件棕色皮衣

一頂具有橘色星星圖標的黑色棒球帽

帶有粉紅色泰迪熊鑰匙圈的一串鑰匙

裝在Hello Kitty卡片夾的一張捷運悠遊卡

一個心型銀色小耳環

一條窄版領帶

請上述物品的失主，至學校D棟辦公室找秘書長珍金斯小姐領回。

<u>重要注意事項</u>

如需領回個人物品，請攜帶一份家長簽名的同意書，確保物歸原主。
10天後，若無人領回上述其一物品，我們將捐贈至慈善機構，幫助無家可歸的小朋友。

謝謝大家
聖誕派對委員會敬上

33《大英百科全書》世上最實用的套書

我們從學會讀寫開始，就會隨時翻閱百科全書來查詢不同主題資訊。其中最聞名的百科全書之一，就是當年於1768年在英國出版的《大英百科全書》。《大英百科全書》起初只是將不同主題的論文集結成冊，而且多數論文均與科學有關。不過，首刷以迅雷不及掩耳的速度售罄後，出版社決定擴大再版的內容幅度。現在，《大英百科全書》網羅了歷史重大事件以及名人軼事。

百科全書曾是傳播歷史科學新知的重要管道。別忘了，人們過去並無法倚賴電腦查詢資訊！提到這個，《大英百科全書》現在亦推出了線上版本，也就是說你可以到圖書館或是隨時隨地使用電子裝置，查詢《大英百科全書》博大精深的知識。

34 冰雪皇后

「有史以來最令人激賞的動人故事。」

—— 吉姆．布朗，《電影雜誌》

「老少咸宜的有趣故事。」

—— 傑瑞．布萊特，《電影脫殼秀》

拉普蘭德是一個永冬之地。每個人自有記憶以來，就只知道冬季的存在。安娜貝爾是名勇敢的農村少女，她決心尋找拉普蘭德冬季永無止盡的原因。在英俊獵人畢格拉夫與其忠犬米特恩的幫助下，安娜貝爾前往冰雪皇后潛居的冰霜山脈，但是路途過程卻驚險萬分。安娜貝爾與朋友們是否能安然穿越嚴寒山區？面對冰雪皇后兇猛的白熊大軍，他們又該如何接招？

絕妙的劇情，彷彿帶領大家踏上拯救王國的魔幻旅程，適合闔家觀賞的趣味情節！

購買《冰雪皇后》藍光光碟，即可一窺許多從未曝光的幕後花絮片段。

此外，藍光光碟還收錄演員專訪、刪除片段以及不同的電影結局版本！

35 可汗學院

一般而言，教師畢生能教導的學生人數能有多少？肯定會有上千人，但不一定能達到上萬人或上百萬人的境界。薩爾曼・可汗也是一名教師，但他的學生卻超過2500萬人。

但單憑一己之力，怎麼有辦法將教學觸角延伸至這麼多人？當然是借助網路的力量。薩爾曼・可汗是「可汗學院」的創辦人，此線上教育機構的宗旨在於為全球各地的任何人，提供免費的世界級教育資訊。

擁有麻省理工學院與哈佛學位的可汗，透過網路擔任表親的數學家教之後，即產生實踐此計畫的念頭。因為可汗的其他親戚也希望得到他的教學幫助，因此他決定自製教學影片並上傳到網路。

可汗學院的網站列有超過2400種的課程教材，科目囊括數學至藝術史。教學格式以YouTube影片呈現，影片最後還會提供若干練習題。

此類教學影片最重要的特色之一，在於不是只有英文的語言選項。可汗學院的課程目前已有65種語言的版本，意即無論使用者的居住地、母語或經濟狀況為何，都可以使用此教學服務。

36 該是離線的時候了

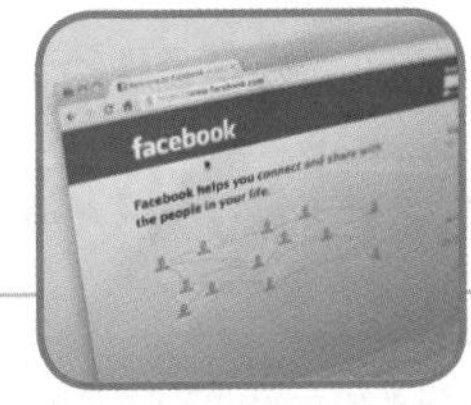

科技探討：該是離線的時候嗎？

作者：R.J.霍華教授

過去幾年以來，科技日新月異的速度令人不可置信。我們現在所處的世界，彷彿各種娛樂資訊和通訊方式，隨時隨地都能在彈指之間完成。但是我們隨身攜帶、可媲美小型電腦的電子裝置，真的有益無害嗎？真的拉近我們與彼此的距離嗎？或是斷送了我們與現實生活接軌的機會？我寫這本書的靈感，來自我的朋友T.M.史塔克教授於2013年底所做的一項實驗。史塔克教授想測驗學生們專心執行某作業的能力，他發現到，經常查看臉書動態的學生，得到的分數較低，而且更難專注於眼前的事務。史塔克教授的研究結果不禁讓我思考：科技到底是讓我們的生活變得更好還是更壞？身為現代科技愛好者的我，有時會覺得難以著手此書內容，撰寫過程亦不好受。不過，我還是毫不掩飾的點出科技的利弊全貌。希望閱讀此書時，讀者也能了解到對科技上癮所能帶來的傷害。

2015年3月

37 馬克・吐溫

馬克・吐溫是美國史上最具文采的知名作家之一。1835年於密蘇里州出生的他，成為作家之前曾任職記者、礦工以及密西西比河的遊輪船長。

他以撰寫《哈克歷險記》而聞名，小說的時空背景設定於美國人仍保有奴隸制度的美國南方地區。故事描述一名少年哈克與逃脫的奴隸吉姆，順著密西西比河展開其冒險旅程。吐溫最令人讚賞的才華之一，就是運用方言的能力，《哈克歷險記》全以美國南方的當地方言撰寫，每個主角均使用生動的語言和口語措詞，因此顯得更加活靈活現。

吐溫亦強烈反對美國社會的許多普遍想法，尤其是種族方面的議題。他藉由小說來抒發自己的見解，雖然已逝於1910年，但馬克・吐溫的著作至今仍十分受歡迎。你或許上英文課時，也讀過他的小說內容，如果是這樣，你一定覺得十分過癮，因為馬克・吐溫說故事的功力可說是一絕！

38 長青科學展

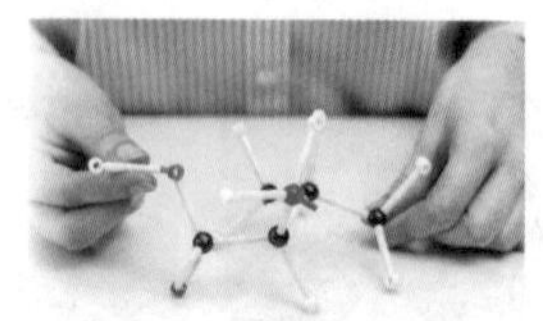

來來來，一同參加
第四屆
長青高中科學展

日期／時間：5月29日，早上9點至下午4點
地點：長青高中體育館

又到了一年一度的科學展！趕緊撢落試管的塵埃，洗淨你的實驗袍，因為長青高中最頂尖聰明的學生們即將來場大對決。今年的主題為「地球上最新一代的厲害能源」。第一名將獲得全新的顯微鏡，還有一個月不用上學的好康（才怪！）；第二名則可贏得長青購物中心價值1000元台幣的禮券。

比賽規則：

1 每位參賽者的作品務必張貼於白色海報，企劃標題必須採用斗大的正楷字體。
2 可於海報上張貼文字敘述與圖片。
3 每項參賽作品務必附有解說企劃內容及其重要原因的文字說明。
4 每項參賽作品必須以學生自行進行的科學實驗為基礎。
5 只要是與參賽者本身的科學實驗有關，即可展示海報以外的道具。
6 家長切勿提供任何協助。

39 魚漿到底是什麼？

我剛翻閱食譜的時候，看到一道令我躍躍欲試的料理：泰式魚餅。看起來真美味，不過，我需要的其中一樣食材叫做fish paste（魚漿），我實在搞不懂這是什麼。我知道電腦術語中的paste是什麼意思，例如「複製貼上」的指令。但這裡的paste是名詞，不是動詞，我想我最好查字典看看。

paste /pest/

名詞

1 濕軟的糊狀混合物體，通常以粉末和液體構成。

2 可抹於麵包或做為烹飪食材的碎肉糊、魚漿等等。

3 將物品黏於紙張的一種漿糊。

4 用於製作仿珠寶（例如鑽石）的一種類玻璃材質。

動詞

1 paste 某物 + 副詞／介係詞——使用膠水或漿糊來將某物黏貼至另一個物品。

2 paste 某物——將數張紙張黏貼在一起而製成某物

3 paste（某物）（電腦術語）——將某處的資訊複製或移動

40 藍色黃金

何謂世上最珍貴的資源？多數人可能會說石油或黃金，其實不然，因為我們無法用石油種植食物，也不需要黃金來維持身體機能。

「水」才是最珍貴的資源，地球有70%的面積都是水，可分配使用的水資源看似豐富，其實只有3%是淡水，供應我們平時農耕、飲食和浴廁方面使用。

約有12億人口已面臨了淡水短缺的問題，到了2025年，此數字預計將增為18億。人口過剩、氣候變遷以及浪費水資源的行為，使短缺問題更加惡化。舉例來說，美國國家環境保護局表示，光是漏水的水龍頭，每年就會浪費掉一兆加侖的水資源，等於洗澡240億次的用水量。

顯而易見，改善此問題人人有責，幸好節約用水並不難。淋浴時間只要減少一分鐘，每個月就能節省150加侖的水；刷牙時關水，一分鐘亦能省下4加侖的水。

41 臉書「打卡」的利弊

智慧型手機與臉書的崛起，改變了人與人之間的互動模式，亦使我們對隱私權的看法產生變化。我們邀請到一位權威來探討臉書「打卡」或發文時附加地點資訊的趨勢。

莎菈：打卡這件事有什麼爭議呢？大家都愛打卡。

約翰：打卡是有很多優點，能讓大家分享自己平時和親友四處遊玩的資訊，也能讓當地生意人藉由網友打卡來替自己打廣告，但是這樣的行為卻需付出隱私權不保的代價。

莎菈：是沒錯，我們已經聽過這樣的說法。但您有發現到，其實自己可以更改臉書設定，控管誰才能看到自己的打卡狀態嗎？

約翰：問題不在這兒，較讓人憂心的是臉書和其他線上公司如何收集你的資訊。如果打卡資訊包括你吃飯、購物與過夜的地點，這就是非常重要的資訊。也許你信任臉書，但是臉書不僅有能力、也絕對會將此類資訊售予你不信任的第三方。

42 名牌仿冒品真的值得購買嗎？

如果我告訴你，你能用比原價低很多的價格買到一項名牌精品，你感興趣嗎？如果我說，雖然不是真品，但外觀和質感幾乎以假亂真，聽起來很超值，不是嗎？

每年都有數十億元的非法名牌仿冒品交易流竄於地下市場。也許你沒有意識到這個問題，但購買LV包包或iPhone的仿冒品，等同此類地下交易的黨羽。

也許你會納悶：「買了名牌仿冒品又如何？沒有妨礙任何人，不是嗎？」結果可能會讓你大吃一驚。

許多名牌仿冒品均於工作環境條件差的血汗工廠所製，裡面的勞工也沒有獲得合理的薪資，某些此類工廠甚至採用童工。此外，憑藉仿冒品大削一筆的人還不用繳稅，使得市立醫院、公立學校以及其他社會機構的政府補助款減少。而且，仿冒品交易的營收通常還會用於支援其他犯罪，包括毒品交易與恐怖主義。

聽起來不再是個好主意了，對吧？

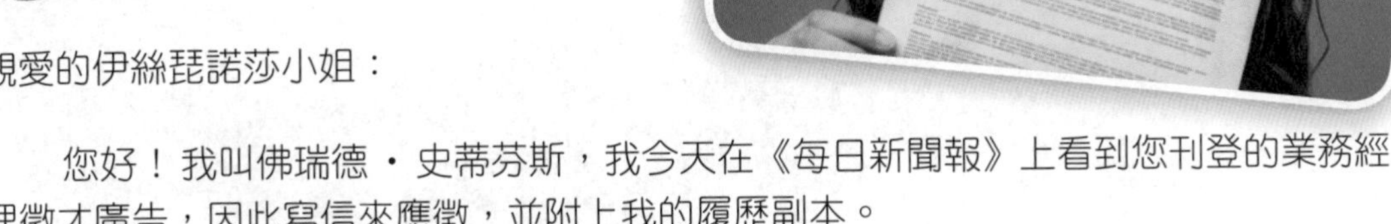

43 電子求職信

親愛的伊絲琵諾莎小姐：

您好！我叫佛瑞德・史蒂芬斯，我今天在《每日新聞報》上看到您刊登的業務經理徵才廣告，因此寫信來應徵，並附上我的履歷副本。

我在2013年以行銷學位畢業於西北大學。畢業後，我一直在舊金山的戴諾晶片電腦公司擔任業務助理。我熱衷自己的工作，工作能力亦獲得讚賞。不過，我真的希望能夠擔任更能掌控會議動態與更常出差的職務。如果能接到更重大的職責，我很確定自己能交出更棒的成績單。此外，我非常希望在歐洲工作，畢業後還曾夢想前往西班牙。我們彼此的工作理念似乎一拍即合，不是嗎？

煩請您盡快回信至我的電子信箱。如果我被錄用，一個月內就能開始上班。您公司所刊登的徵才廣告似乎是令人雀躍的工作機會，我真的非常希望自己能拔得頭籌。

感謝您撥冗看信，希望您有個美好的一天！

祝安康

佛瑞德・史蒂芬斯

44 世界地球日

我們每年都會聽到此名詞，但是到底何謂世界地球日？每逢4月22日，就是響應世界地球日的時刻，目的在於多加關懷環境議題，以及人類的行為對環境造成何種影響。現在將近200個國家落實此活動，其起源始於1970年，當時是為了教導美國學生瞭解環境保護的重要性。往後的20年左右，該活動幾乎遭人遺忘，卻以不同凡響的方式捲土重來。

1990年的「世界地球日20周年慶」，帶動141個國家超過2億人口留意此盛事。此現象讓全球各地的政府意識到資源回收的重要性，並使環保議題受到國際關注。世界地球日也因而成為一年一度的活動，而非每十年舉辦一次。2000年的世界地球日規模更加盛大，183個國家中，有超過5000個團體響應。網路世界是該次活動的主要統籌工具，而電影明星李奧納多・狄卡皮歐更擔任活動主持人。

不過，有些人認為將4月22日選做世界地球日，足以顯見共產黨的影響力。因為1970年4月22日是蘇聯領導人列寧的100年誕辰紀念日。不過，世界地球日的意義現已超越政治，而且是國際間少數取得協議共識的活動。

45 半人半鳥

極限運動的最新熱潮，是將人類不可能像鳥類般飛翔的落差化為可能，此活動稱為「飛鼠裝滑翔運動」，也可說是全世界最危險的運動。

飛鼠裝滑翔運動歸類為定點跳傘運動，意指玩家從高空物體或高處跳傘，差別在於使用的裝備。飛鼠裝滑翔運動好手的裝備於手腳間均有增加迎風面積的翅膜，這種增加的翅膜可產生拉力，讓玩家飛行數分鐘之久再以降落傘著地。飛鼠裝滑翔運動玩家於空中飛行的模樣十分與眾不同，有人說看似蝙蝠，有人說看似疾速拯救世界的超級英雄。

與其他極限運動一樣，飛鼠裝滑翔運動吸引玩家的是刺激感。不過，水可載舟亦可覆舟，學習飛鼠裝滑翔運動的過程中，沒有犯錯的空間，只要一個錯誤，就可能天人永隔，例如此運動佼佼者迪恩・波特的遭遇，2015年5月，迪恩於美國優勝美地國家公園跳傘時不幸喪生。

46 網路購書

《古希臘的故事》

作者：
麥克・川特與茂德・連姆

平均評價：★★★★

馬上購入

數量 1

電子書 $10.99

實體書 $12.99

加入購物車

古希臘的輝煌事蹟可說是史上最令人激賞的動聽故事，情節以善妒神祇與驍勇英雄之間產生的愛情、引發的戰爭以及各種魔法交織而成。雋永的故事上千年來令大家津津樂道，更影響了西方世界的某些偉大作家。

大家可在麥克・川特的這本新著作，看到鐵修斯、柏修斯、柏勒洛豐與海克力斯等屠殺怪獸的英雄故事，皮拉穆斯與提絲蓓、奧菲斯與尤麗狄絲的愛情故事，還有阿基里斯、赫克特與奧德賽等特洛伊戰爭偉大戰士的故事，族繁不及備載。

川特以戲劇化的生動措詞重述古希臘故事，讓二十一世紀的讀者有幸瞭解古希臘的世界。

而畫家茂德・連姆一系列的美麗素描與水彩插畫，更讓故事內容栩栩如生。

47 耀眼的山景

台中市的大雪山社區以可口水果與美麗的油桐花聞名。不過，令全台民眾慕名而來的另一大雪山美景，則非螢火蟲莫屬。

五月是大雪山的螢火蟲季，夕陽西下後，整片山頭都被小光點般四處飄移的螢火蟲覆蓋，這樣的美景令人屏息，每年也吸引了上千名遊客來到這小原住民社區。觀光活動帶動了大雪山的經濟發展，讓仍因集集大地震而重建家園的居民受惠。

大雪山完全是自然環境與人類生計之間取得平衡的最佳範本。大家致力保護這片淨土，確保遊客不會留下任何損害。螢火蟲季期間，整個大雪山社區均為熄燈狀態，連汽車大燈都不能開，遊客必須在距離賞螢景點1300公尺處下車步行至目的地。欣賞螢火蟲之美的同時，亦需遵守「五不規定」：不追逐、不捕捉、不靠近棲息地、不大聲喧嘩且不能點燈。

48 會呼吸的道路

多數科學家均認同，未來的氣候型態只會越來越難預料。意思是全球將面臨更多風暴、水災與旱災的問題。幸好，已有不少人研發令人耳目一新的方法，來因應此新常態現象。

陳瑞文就是其中一人。他發明的JW生態鋪路工法，讓道路具有海綿般的吸水滲透力。當水分觸及這種「會呼吸的道路」時，路面下的小型塑膠導水管就能即時吸水，再透過底下的碎石層達到淨水作用，往地表流動形成大型的臨時水庫，供未來利用。如此一來，就能汲收和儲存雨水，遇到乾旱氣候時即可發揮效用。

JW生態鋪路工法的優點非僅止於此，還能吸熱、防止積雪，甚至清淨空汙，更不需要特別的養護。

台北市汐止區與多處已鋪設了會呼吸的道路。陳瑞文相信，這樣的鋪路工法很快就會席捲全球。短期來說，或許造價不斐，但長遠來看，卻能因為預防代價龐大的水災而節省不少費用。

49 特洛伊木馬

病毒、蠕蟲、特洛伊木馬——上述程式都會對電腦造成嚴重傷害。特洛伊木馬程式防不勝防，因為剛開始總是以無害的形式出現。特洛伊木馬程式可能會喬裝為電子信箱附件或看似有趣的下載檔案，一旦進入電腦，就會開始竊取所有的個人資料或刪除所有檔案。

不過，「特洛伊木馬」此名詞到底從何而來？相傳很久以前，希臘與特洛伊城之間掀起一場戰爭，特洛伊城的城牆高聳又堅而不摧，希臘人苦無攻城之計，戰爭持續了十年，希臘人終於想出法子。他們建造了一匹巨大木馬，並讓士兵躲於其中，再佯裝乘船返鄉。特洛伊人以為打贏戰爭，將木馬運入城內慶祝勝利。當晚，木馬內的士兵破繭而出，大開城門，其他的希臘軍隊早已悄悄返回特洛伊，因此趁機攻打而摧毀了特洛伊城。

注意

過去三週以來，本社區已接獲數起自行車失竊的通報情況。第一起失竊案發生於查爾斯頓路和車隊街的交叉街角，有四部自行車遭竊；最近一起則於上週末發生，麥迪遜路上某住戶停放於車庫的自行車遭竊。

有兩大原因，顯示這幾起竊案互有關聯。第一，我們都知道，在這個平靜的社區，自行車失竊是前所未有的事，接二連三發生這樣的事，表示社區內出現了「老鼠屎」，目前已有人目擊這幾起竊案。

如果您見到長得像此公告的人，請立刻聯絡社區委員會或報警。我們衷心希望逮捕此竊賊，也會派人24小時接聽熱線電話。社區的保全巡邏隊亦將定時勘查守望，每位警衛均持有嫌犯的圖像。

以下為目擊者所描述的嫌犯特點：

- 男性，身高約180公分
- 留著一頭及肩黑色長髮
- 其中一名目擊者表示「嫌犯皮膚泛紅」
- 最近一次被目擊身穿黑色牛仔褲、黑色運動衫且戴墨鏡

In Focus 英語閱讀 3
活用五大關鍵技巧

發行人	黃朝萍
作者	Owain Mckimm / Zachary Fillingham / Shara Dupuis / Richard Luhrs
譯者	劉嘉珮
審訂	Richard Luhrs
編輯	丁宥暄
企畫編輯	葉俞均
封面設計	林書玉
內頁設計	鄭秀芳／林書玉（中譯解答）
製程管理	洪巧玲
出版者	寂天文化事業股份有限公司
電話	02-2365-9739
傳真	02-2365-9835
網址	www.icosmos.com.tw
讀者服務	onlineservice@icosmos.com.tw
出版日期	2023年3月 初版再刷 （寂天雲隨身聽APP版）(0102)
郵撥帳號	1998620-0 寂天文化事業股份有限公司

訂書金額未滿1000元，請外加運費100元。
〔若有破損，請寄回更換，謝謝〕

國家圖書館出版品預行編目資料

In Focus英語閱讀 3：活用五大關鍵技巧（寂天雲隨身聽APP版）/ Owain Mckimm等著；劉嘉珮譯. -- 初版. -- [臺北市]：寂天文化, 2022.08
面；　公分
ISBN 978-626-300-151-0(16K平裝)
1.CST: 英語 2.CST: 讀本
805.18　　111012599

ANSWERS

1	**1.** b	**2.** c	**3.** a	**4.** a	**5.** d
2	**1.** b	**2.** d	**3.** c	**4.** d	**5.** b
3	**1.** c	**2.** a	**3.** d	**4.** c	**5.** b
4	**1.** c	**2.** d	**3.** b	**4.** c	**5.** c
5	**1.** b	**2.** d	**3.** b	**4.** a	**5.** a

6	**1.** c	**2.** d	**3.** c	**4.** b	**5.** b
7	**1.** d	**2.** c	**3.** b	**4.** b	**5.** a
8	**1.** c	**2.** b	**3.** d	**4.** a	**5.** b
9	**1.** d	**2.** c	**3.** a	**4.** c	**5.** d
10	**1.** a	**2.** c	**3.** b	**4.** d	**5.** c

11	**1.** b	**2.** d	**3.** a	**4.** b	**5.** c
12	**1.** c	**2.** b	**3.** a	**4.** b	**5.** c
13	**1.** d	**2.** c	**3.** a	**4.** b	**5.** c
14	**1.** d	**2.** b	**3.** a	**4.** c	**5.** b
15	**1.** a	**2.** c	**3.** c	**4.** b	**5.** a

16	**1.** c	**2.** d	**3.** a	**4.** c	**5.** b
17	**1.** d	**2.** a	**3.** a	**4.** c	**5.** a
18	**1.** b	**2.** a	**3.** c	**4.** b	**5.** c
19	**1.** c	**2.** c	**3.** b	**4.** b	**5.** b
20	**1.** c	**2.** a	**3.** b	**4.** d	**5.** c

21	**1.** b	**2.** a	**3.** b	**4.** c	**5.** a
22	**1.** c	**2.** d	**3.** c	**4.** a	**5.** a
23	**1.** d	**2.** a	**3.** b	**4.** a	**5.** a
24	**1.** d	**2.** b	**3.** c	**4.** a	**5.** c
25	**1.** a	**2.** b	**3.** a	**4.** c	**5.** d

26	1. d	2. d	3. a	4. d	5. a
27	1. a	2. d	3. b	4. d	5. c
28	1. b	2. a	3. c	4. d	5. b
29	1. b	2. d	3. d	4. c	5. a
30	1. a	2. b	3. c	4. d	5. c

31	1. b	2. c	3. d	4. a	5. b
32	1. c	2. d	3. c	4. a	5. a
33	1. c	2. c	3. d	4. c	5. a
34	1. d	2. b	3. a	4. c	5. c
35	1. c	2. b	3. b	4. a	5. d

36	1. c	2. b	3. d	4. a	5. b
37	1. b	2. b	3. c	4. a	5. d
38	1. b	2. a	3. c	4. b	5. d
39	1. d	2. b	3. a	4. b	5. a
40	1. b	2. d	3. b	4. b	5. a

41	1. b	2. b	3. c	4. a	5. b
42	1. c	2. d	3. b	4. d	5. d
43	1. c	2. a	3. d	4. c	5. b
44	1. d	2. b	3. d	4. c	5. a
45	1. d	2. c	3. b	4. d	5. b

46	1. d	2. c	3. b	4. a	5. b
47	1. c	2. a	3. b	4. d	5. b
48	1. b	2. b	3. a	4. a	5. b
49	1. c	2. d	3. c	4. b	5. a
50	1. d	2. d	3. b	4. a	5. a